Happily
Ever After
This Christmas

C.K. Martin

Published by Rogue Hedgehog Media

Copyright © 2017 C.K. Martin

All rights reserved.

ISBN-13: 9781973379928

CONTENTS

CHAPTER ONE

An old-fashioned bell tinkled above the door as it opened. Kayleigh looked up automatically. Johnson's Independent Bookstore had been her second home since she was so young that the bell had trained her better than one of Pavlov's dogs. Two young people came through, talking in a language that she couldn't understand, but could still hear the wonder. She smiled, doubtful they would buy anything, but happy they had walked through the door anyway.

As she laid out more books on the front table — a surprise hit from an author presumed past her sell-by date was an ongoing task — she looked out into the street. It was still busy out there, the coach party of elderly Christmas shoppers not yet quite ready to leave.

Kayleigh finished stacking the books and made her way back down the aisle, automatically straightening spines as she went. Tinsel made the task slower compared to normal, but it also made it special. It was hard work to decorate the store for Christmas each year, but it was always worth it in the end.

It had been her grandfather, the original owner of the bookstore, who had insisted on the Christmas displays. Back then, owning a bookstore in a quiet little town in the English Cotswolds wasn't the most financially viable option, but the tourist industry had helped them continue to survive the many economic ups and downs throughout the years. Now it was all hers. The displays had grown bigger and she tried to tell herself it wasn't overcompensating for the fact she was doing it all alone.

Many of the other shops along the high street had moved with the times. They had modernised the layout, with light and airy spaces that would work well for local magazine photos, should they ever have the good fortune of being featured. Along with the light, soft pine tables, they had severely pared down their stock; trinkets and fashion were the name of the game when you wanted to sell to the ever-changing tourist market. Those shops, despite being in the majority, were not shops for locals. The names may have been handed down for generations, but the ethos hadn't.

Kayleigh had refused to do the same with Johnson's Books. Her family hadn't worked hard to build the collection from the ground up just so she could sell novelty pens and gifts. It was a bookstore and it should remain a bookstore. The locals still used it and, despite the different marketing logic, the tourists seemed to love it too. When you have travelled halfway around the world to see quaint little old England, she realised, then it shouldn't feel like you could be in McAnywhere.

Instead, the dark wooden bookshelves lined the walls, crammed with books from all genres, all eras. Kayleigh wanted it to be a place you could come to enjoy finding a book. Any book, not just the ones that happened to be in the top fifty at any given moment. Her only concession had been the addition, towards the front of the store, of two dark olive armchairs and a small table. She hadn't gone quite as far as serving coffee yet, despite many requests that she do so, not to mention her own desire to have it on hand throughout the day. If sales fell too much, then there may be no choice but to capitulate. For now though, the many tea rooms along the street could cater to the caffeine and sugar cravings of her patrons. Besides, sticky fingers on books were more likely to be damaging to business than the loss of an occasional sale.

Bright white fairy lights gave an extra seasonal brightness, but although the two tourists picked up many things, they ultimately walked out empty handed, as she'd known they would. She could read people by now, not quite as well as the books on the shelves, but close. Over the coming week, the true build up to Christmas would begin and she wouldn't have time to people watch. It would be all hands to the pump as people took advantage of the 'two for one' offers and the wider selection of new releases that came with this time of year. Kayleigh couldn't wait. The busy, 'rushed off her feet until she was ready to drop' feeling left her too tired at the end of the day to even think. Sometimes, that was a place she needed to be.

Another soft tinkle came from the front of the store and she turned to look back. A woman walked through the door and Kayleigh sized her up, unable to put immediately place her into one of the categories she had created over the years for just that purpose. She didn't seem familiar. Kayleigh knew most of the locals by sight, one way or another. When you're tied to a village, you made yourself an integral part of it if you wanted to survive. Who you knew, rather than what you knew, was the currency of choice. She'd drawn the line at joining the Women's Institute, like her mother before her. That was a level of commitment to tradition she wasn't quite prepared to sacrifice herself to just yet. Besides, cooking had never really been her thing. She could tell you about Blake's *Jerusalem* but she couldn't make jam.

The woman tilted her head towards the empty counter, noting the lack of anyone there to help her before her eyes scanned the room. No, she wasn't a local, but she wasn't a tourist either. However she was, a traitorous voice whispered inside Kayleigh's brain, cute. She shook the thought away. She didn't have time for cute. Especially not with the festivities about to get underway. Cute could wait for spring, like it always did. Or the season after that.

Confident that her face wouldn't give her away, she put on her best smile and walked towards the door. She noticed a Hemingway had been half pulled out by a previous customer and her hand smoothed the spine back into line in a single fluid action as she walked past. 'Can I help you?'

'Hi. Yes. Perhaps? I'm looking for the owner.'

'That's me.'

'Oh.' The woman looked surprised and Kayleigh tried not to bristle. Perhaps thirty-four was a tender age to own a place like this, but that was more circumstance than entirely of her own choosing. Not that the woman extending her hand needed to know that. Extending her hand? Things suddenly seemed terribly formal. 'Jo Pearmain. I work for the council.'

'Oh.' It was Kayleigh's turn to be confused. In all the years she had been in the bookstore, even as a teenager forced to work the Saturday shift, or after school, she couldn't recall them ever getting a visit from the council. 'What can I do for you?'

'I'm with the Health and Safety team.' The woman who had introduced herself as Jo fumbled in her pocket, pulling out an ID badge. Kayleigh peered at it. The picture was surprisingly flattering. However, she couldn't really take in the dark brown eyes that under normal circumstances would have made her think of hot chocolate. Instead, it was the department logo, stamped at the top, which gave her pause. This could not be good.

'Health and Safety? I check the paperwork every January. I'm up to date with everything.'

'I'm afraid,' said Jo, voice formal and stern enough to be a school mistress, not a council lackey, 'I'm going to have to look at that.'

The moment the words came tumbling out, Kayleigh didn't even need to follow the direction of the finger that Jo was pointing. The Christmas display at the back of the shop filled the entire of the back alcove. A smaller section of the store that due to the layout of the staircase behind, formed a narrow, smaller 'room' at the back. It was the ideal place to put the display, out of the way of the customers who came in looking for presents. If someone wanted an actual book from that section, where the large fir touched the ceiling and also the shelves in places, then Kayleigh could find it for them. She knew every inch of the shelves by heart. It just took a small amount of nimble contortion to get to them, that was all.

'The display?'

'Yes.'

'It's only temporary.'

'I would imagine it is.' Sturdy silence. The woman wasn't going to back down and go on her merry way. Kayleigh would have no choice but to show her.

The display was the heart of the shop at Christmas. Whilst tinsel and fairy lights adorned bookshelves and tables, the tree at the back of the store was the *pièce de résistance*. Swathes of red and gold, ornaments new and old, filled its branches and brought the old building to life. She had deliberately made it as old-fashioned as she could, taking her cues from Christmas biscuit tins and Dickens. It never changed with the latest Christmas fashions; its branches simply grew heavier each year with items that she had found, or had been donated by a friendly local trying to get rid of things so they could move with the times themselves.

For the first time, she looked at it with a more critical eye. Perhaps the locals had donated a *few* too many things. They'd all been so sweet in their generosity that Kayleigh had been unable to say no to anything. As the woman stood there in silence, it became apparent that she wasn't going to be the first person she said no to either. 'I suppose you want to take a look at it?'

'I'm going to have to.'

'Follow me.' Kayleigh crossed her fingers and hoped that no one she knew would come into the shop and witness what was going on. Or worse, a swathe of customers that meant she would have to leave Miss Whateverhername was alone. The quicker they could get this over with, the better.

As they drew up to the tree, Kayleigh saw it with a newly critical eye that had nothing to do with artistic merit. All the little things that would have made it fine in her own home were not going to cut it here. She braced herself for the questions. Then considered the supreme alternative: distraction. 'Can I get you something to drink, er...' damn what was the woman's name again?

'Jo.'

'Yes. Jo. Tea? Coffee?'

'I'm fine thank you.' Jo fished around in her bag and pulled out a small notebook. As she opened it to the next blank page, Kayleigh tried to work out the scribbles that had preceded it. She needed to know how ruthless a health and safety inspector this woman was. She thought she knew everyone who had lived around here long enough to hold a position that came with any kind of clout, but apparently not. The words, never in complete sentences, were indecipherable. Then she found the next page and began the inspection. 'Is the tree secured in any fashion?'

'Secured?'

'Yes. Secured. To prevent it from toppling?'

'It's in a really big pot.' Kayleigh pointed. It was pretty big.

'So the pot is secured? To the floor or another surface?'

'No.'

'I see.' Jo scribbled something that looked like 'mango'. Kayleigh was baffled. This woman had worse handwriting than she did.

'But everyone knows not to go past it. If they need a book from that section, then I go and get it for them.'

'I see. So you accept that it is a potential hazard?'

'Hazard is such a strong word. I just know where things are most likely to fall off.' As soon as the words were out of her mouth she regretted them. Things falling off were the same as a hazard to a person like Jo. Her heart sank as another scribble hit the page.

'So no members of the public are given access to this alcove?'

'No. Not while the display is up. That's only three weeks each year. It's not really a problem for the business.'

'Only three weeks? I thought everyone put their Christmas displays up in October these days?' Jo looked genuinely surprised. Perhaps she thought she was lying to make the problem seem less than it was.

'Yes, just three weeks. It's for—'

'But you don't have anything specifically designed to prevent any members of the public coming back here?'

'What do you mean?'

'No ropes? Warning signs?'

'Well, no. But I make it very clear to them.'

'Verbally?'

'Yes.' This was getting ridiculous now. If there were no signs or ropes but she made it clear to them, then how else was she going to do it? Telepathy?

'What if you are busy with a customer?'

'I call across to them. If I see them heading down that way.'

'So you are reliant on being able to see them and communicate with them personally. There are no other members of staff?'

'Sometimes. In the busy periods.' That wasn't a lie. She had one or two helpers. Part time employees. Mainly Saturday girls, as she still called them.

'So no one here to act as a permanent deterrent?'

'Deterrent? That's a bit dramatic isn't it?' Again, Kayleigh's brain willed the words back a few seconds too late.

'I have to take this seriously. If there is an active risk to the public, then it is my job to make sure that they are protected.'

'Of course.' This time, the words, *of course you do, who shoved that rod up your backside?* actually stayed in her head, locked behind the sweetest smile-grimace her face could manage. 'I'm sure I could get something to act as a deterrent. Most of the books there are only of interest to the locals anyway. They know better than to try and get to them.'

'I see.' Another cryptic scribble. 'Is there anything else you wish to tell me before I investigate further?'

'I don't think so.' Everything she'd said so far had only incriminated her further, so Kayleigh decided this might be a good time to actually keep her mouth shut. She was about to issue another offer of a drink, when the tinkle above the door reached her ears. Damn. She was going to have to leave this woman to her own devices and hope that nothing went wrong. Well, any more wrong than it already had.

'I'm just going to see this customer.'

'That's fine. I'll let you know when I'm done.' The woman crouched down, looking under the display. If she was hoping to find presents there, then she was going to be sorely disappointed. Santa didn't come to this tree. Not yet.

Kayleigh wandered to the front of the store to check on things. She recognised the balding head of one of her regulars, in every Monday and Thursday. He seldom purchased anything, but she was sure he had read the blurb on the back of every single cover by now. Over the years, she had tried and failed to get him to reveal what kind of thing he was actually looking for. He was a man of few purchases but of many words. As always, she put on her best smile and walked over to him. Usually it was genuine, but with a health and safety inspector on the loose, then it was hard to give him her full attention.

*

Dusk had given way to complete darkness, making the wood in the shop appear even more antique. The decorations never gave the full feeling of a traditional English Christmas until night came around. The after school rush was over. Soon the kids would break up for the holidays and they would be in the shop more and more during the day, buying Christmas presents for parents.

Only a handful bought books for friends these days. The ones that did were often the ones she ended up giving the part time jobs to.

Other than to check once that Jo was okay and didn't need anything further, Kayleigh had resisted the urge to hover over her. The woman was determined to do a thorough job and the more Kayleigh tried to stop her from seeing, the more she looked for. It was a no win situation. Instead, she had to simply wait for the verdict.

The verdict was on a three page form. Jo handed it to her as she stood at the counter, the two feet of thick wood acting as a barrier to stop her from reaching out and physically assaulting the woman as she saw a litany of scribbles — slightly neater than the ones in the notebook, no references to mangos anywhere — covering the page. 'So what does this mean?' she asked, not wanting to know.

'I'll talk you through it.'

'Please do.'

'A few of the things we have already discussed. The tree itself needs to be secured. Not all trees need to be, but given its height and erm, extensive contents, this one does.'

'I see.' That surely could be sorted easily enough. She wasn't sure how yet, but the DIY superstore in the next town along would most likely have something she could use.

'Some of the objects on the tree's branches are quite heavy and placed at height.' The woman read from the list like an automaton. Kayleigh loved her job, even on the darkest and loneliest of days, but she'd never felt this grateful for it before. Imagine having to do this for a living instead? It took a special kind of soulless person to do this to someone at Christmas.

'Which means?' Kayleigh realised the woman had trailed of and was looking at her, presumably waiting for some kind of response.

'Which means they could pose a falling risk. Especially

to any children in the area.'

'I told you, no one goes into the area.'

'Because of a verbal warning, correct?'

'Yes.' She already knew where this was going. Another thing she could predict was a large glass of wine in her future when this was all done.

'I'm afraid that is insufficient Ms Johnson.'

'So what do I need?'

'I'm afraid you need to close off the area to the public. A rope barrier should be sufficient. A warning sign would also be advantageous, but shouldn't be used in place of the rope.'

'Surely a warning sign would be enough? A rope will make it look a lot less welcoming.'

'A warning sign is reliant on people being able to read.'

'It's a book shop. If they've come in here looking for something, it's a pretty good bet they can read.'

'This is serious.' The stern look was back again, although for a second Kayleigh was sure she saw a twinkle of amusement in the other woman's eyes. If it was there, it was gone as soon as it had come.

'Okay, okay. So I'll get some kind of warning sign and a rope put up. Will that do? Where do I sign to say I'll get on with it?'

'I'm afraid there's more.'

'Seriously?'

'I wish that was it. I don't enjoy having to be the one to do this.'

'I'm sure you don't.' Kayleigh could hear the spite in her own voice and the woman's face hardened again. Damn. She'd made it worse. A sinking feeling came over her. Whatever was coming next wasn't going to be good.

'We need to discuss your electrical set up.'

'Electrical…' There it was. Kayleigh's heart sunk like a stone. Minor infractions were an annoyance. Major ones could shut down an actual business for weeks. She knew of one of the locals who had almost lost their livelihoods one summer. The old buildings on the high street brought with them traditional character, but that came with structural issues all the time. She couldn't afford to have the store closed down on health and safety grounds during the busiest period of the year for her.

'Yes, electrical.' Jo looked at her notepad again as if to remind herself of the facts. 'You've got too many lights using extension cables.'

'Is that all? I can turn the lights off.' Kayleigh breathed a sigh of relief. It wouldn't be quite the same as a beautifully lit giant tree, but it wasn't the end of the world.

'Which made me realise that the sockets you were using weren't up to code in that part of the building.'

'Ah.' Oh yes. That. A job she had been meaning to get done for quite a while. The alcove was technically powered by the older part of the building that served as an office, but wasn't strictly part of the shop. Her grandfather had interpreted that, she had discovered one winter evening when the power tripped, as a nice technicality to effectively halve the cost of the shop rewire. It worked fine. So fine, in fact, that she was able to make sure the task of getting it fixed remained permanently at the bottom of her to do list. A tree without lights wasn't pretty, but a tree in total darkness was something else entirely. Even in summer, the bright natural light from outside couldn't penetrate that part of the bookstore. She'd need a torch if someone wanted an item from the shelves.

'Does that mean you knew it was a problem?' The woman's pen was hovering over the form. Kayleigh swallowed. It felt like a trap. She knew it was a problem before she put the tree up, somewhere in her awareness. But it wasn't like she had remembered and then actively flouted the rules in the hope of getting away with it. She simply had too much on this time of year to remember trivialities like local government codes. Her mouth opened, her brain still grasping for the correct reply. When none came, she closed it again, do her best impression of a dying salmon. Panic began to take over. She looked at Jo again. Their eyes locked. Then almost imperceptibly, there was a slight shake of the head.

Was she telling her to say no? Kayleigh was confused. Without seeing the forms, she had no idea of the consequences of saying yes. It wouldn't be a lie, exactly. Yes, it would. The twin voices of guilt and self-preservation argued in her head. It had seemed like a shake of the head. An insignificant twitch that was enough to let self-preservation win the argument. 'No?' It came out as more of a question than a statement. A flicker of a smile on Jo's face and she placed a cross through one of the boxes.

'That's good to know. Deliberate infringements are viewed quite harshly. There can be additional fines if done with intent.'

'Definitely no intent here.' This time, with a cost associated with the answer, it was much easier to issue a denial. Cash flow was always tight. The slush fund she kept for emergencies such as this wouldn't stretch to an additional fine. It would barely stretch to cover the cost of getting the issue fixed. She hoped.

'At least the front half of the shop is up to code. Which means I won't be issuing you a notice to cease trading. I'm afraid that the back half of the shop will be out of bounds until it gets resolved. Lights and sockets.'

'You mean I can't just turn the extension leads off and carry on with things how they normally are?'

'No. In the interests of public health and safety, I can't allow that to happen until there has been a re-inspection confirming you are up to code.'

'A re-inspection? At this time of year? What are the chances of me getting one of those?' The sinking feeling was beginning to take hold. Getting an electrician to take on a big job at this time of year was going to be tough enough. Getting someone from the council to come back out on an unscheduled job wasn't going to happen until the New Year. By then, it would be too late. The tears began to well up in her eyes and she clenched her jaw tight together in a bid to stop them from brimming over. She wasn't prone to crying at the slightest thing, but at this time of year…

'Given the nature of the incident, we will do everything we can to ensure that a re-inspection happens in a timely manner. But I can't make any promises.'

'Of course you can't.'

'I wish there was something else I could do.'

'You don't care. If you did, then you would let me sort it out after Christmas like a decent person.'

'Ms Johnson, may I remind you that I am well within my rights to shut down your entire operation if I deem it to be dangerous to the general public. Your *entire* operation.' She looked meaningfully around the rest of the shop. 'I am letting you off on a technicality, but if you want me to begin my inspection again and reassess, I am more than willing to?'

'No, that won't be necessary.' Kayleigh deflated. There was no argument she could win here. She was, after all, in the wrong and she knew it. If it hadn't been this year, then another would have passed without her thinking about it. She'd never had any trouble with the council before. It was just her here now and when you worked alone, then only the urgent jobs tended to get done. Better now, she supposed, than before the whole place was set on fire by one set of fairy lights too many.

'Good. Here are your copies of the forms.' Jo tore off the top copy and handed it over. She fished around in her bag and pulled out a small paper rectangle. 'Here's my card. It's got my office number and my mobile number on it. When you get the work done, if you call me directly I will do what I can to get the visit prioritised. If you just call the main office, it will go to the bottom of the list. That's about the best I can do I'm afraid.'

'Fine.' Kayleigh didn't take the offer in good grace. Her

better nature was refusing to come out to play, even though she supposed the card was meant to be an olive branch. She snatched it from Jo's hand and shoved it into the back pocket of her jeans without even reading it. When she looked back up, Jo's face was once again hard and distant. Kayleigh knew she was blowing chances left right and centre, but she didn't care. One small crack in her walls today and the whole thing would come tumbling down. 'Are you done? I need to close up.'

'Yes. Thank you for your time.'

'Oh, the pleasure was all mine.' Sarcasm was the intent, but maliciousness undercut the humour. 'I'll be in touch.'

Kayleigh watched as Jo stuffed her things in her bag and moved to the front of the store. She paused, for a second, to look at something on one of the shelves. Then she was gone, opening and closing the door to the tinkling of a bell that sounded so forlorn that it prompted more tears.

This time, Kayleigh just let them fall.

CHAPTER TWO

Jo twisted the key in the lock, a once reflex action that was now coming back to her. The door popped open and a welcome rush of heat met her. She slipped inside and closed it behind her, leaning back against the wood. That had to go down as the worst day of the new job so far.

Gently, so as not to attract attention, she banged the back of her head against the door several times. This was a nightmare. An absolute living nightmare. Proof that life could turn on a dime as her father would say, even though he had never been to America and had probably never seen a dime. Too many bloody westerns on TV when he was growing up most likely.

Speaking of which, the house was in silence. The lights were on and the heating was most definitely on, but there were no other noises. Panic reared its ugly head and she set off to the living room without removing her boots.

Jo pushed open the door, her brain preparing her to see images of her father lying there on the floor, helpless. Worse, dead. Guilt images, she knew that. Ones she had conjured up for herself a million times in the last two months. She shot through the door and looked at the floor.

Nothing.

As her eyes swivelled to her father's chair, he looked at her quizzically, pausing his crossword. The pencil hovered mid-air as he tried not to smile. Clearly she looked like a possessed lunatic. 'And how are you?' he asked. He looked her up and down, taking in the coat and boots that were usually left at the front door.

'It was quiet in here.' A bit of a non-sequitur response.

'I'm doing the crossword. The TV was distracting me so I turned it off. That's not a crime is it?'

'Sorry. I was just worried.'

'Well go and get out of those damp clothes or there will be two of us you have to worry about.'

'Yes Dad.' Feeling foolish that she had once again over-reacted, she left the man to his crossword and traipsed back out into the hall. Taking off the professional coat and boots, she began to feel her true self start to emerge. The bottom of her trousers felt damp and she knew her father was right. This sort of weather seeped into everything. She set off up the stairs she had climbed a thousand times as a teenager, but perhaps not more than a dozen since she had left for university. Up until the last few weeks, that was.

In her old bedroom, she threw off her clothes and pulled on the comforting warmth of an old pair of jeans and a festive jumper. Boxes, still unpacked, blocked her way to the bookcase, but she looked at it, trying to imagine what it must be like to own your own bookstore. It felt like a fairytale and she had been the villain in that story today. She closed her eyes in frustration again and headed down the stairs.

She made two cups of tea and placed one on the tray that sat atop of the walking aid her father was supposed to use. 'Here you go.'

'Thanks, Love. How was your day?'

'Finish your crossword first.' It wasn't really an act of generosity. Jo simply needed another moment before she could even begin to verbalise how her day was. How could she say to the man in front of her that it was the kind of day that made her want to pack her bags and leave all over again?

'The crossword can wait until tomorrow. When I spend most of my day alone, why do something like that when I've got some company? Besides, I've been stuck on sixteen down for an hour now.'

'Do you want me to help?'

'No thanks young lady. It's my body that's gone, not my mind. You start doing the crosswords for me and it'll be sure to follow, mark my words.'

'I'm not sure my brain would be of any use to you today anyway.'

'You look tired.'

'Yes, that's all it is.'

'You need a break. Why don't you go away for the weekend? I can manage.'

'No, that's okay. This close to Christmas everyone will already have plans. I'm just going to have a lazy day here instead. Perhaps unpack the rest of the boxes in my room.' She plastered on a bright smile. It sounded plausible to her own ears. Whether or not she would fool him was a different matter.

Her father was right, he still had all his mental faculties. For that, she was infinitely grateful on a daily basis. But when it came to his own physical capabilities, he remained wilfully optimistic. To the point, she knew, of delusion. He hated using his walking trolley. The first time he had seen it, he had taken one look at the table at the top — a feature she had thought was a particularly nice touch — and asked if she had stolen it from IKEA.

It wasn't that he was antagonistic about it. She knew he wasn't being a pain in the arse for the sake of it. Although he had his moments, he was still the same father he had been all her life. He hadn't mellowed, but he hadn't turned into a cantankerous old man either. He was just unable to be realistic about his fate. Perhaps if she had been around, she would have been able to suggest the trolley aid a while back. Then he might never have taken the tumble that brought her back here for good.

'Well, if you're going to be around,' he continued, reaching out and taking his cup of tea, 'perhaps you wouldn't mind picking up a thing or two for me from the village?'

'Of course I wouldn't.'

'It gets harder to get presents every year. I have no idea what to get you these days.'

'You don't have to get me anything.'

'Of course I do. You might be too old for Santa now, but you're not too old for presents. Have a think about it. Give the old man a few ideas.'

'Don't you want to come with me? We could go together and you could take a look for yourself.'

'In that contraption? You won't be able to get around with it this time of year.' He didn't have to specify which contraption he was talking about. The wheelchair. The public symbol of his fall into frailty and away from being the strapping man he once was. Since she had returned, she had taken him out in it a handful of times. She couldn't say it had been a particularly pleasant experience for either of them. She was not, as it turned out, a natural wheelchair pusher. Just as much as he wasn't one of life's natural patients.

Yet here they were. Stuck with each other.

Jo pushed the thought away. It had been her choice to return to look after him. The broken hip was a sign she simply couldn't ignore. So many weekends had slipped by with the promise of a visit that never came. She was young. She had a social life. She had escaped the small town she had grown up in and vowed never to come back to. The fall had changed all that. Without a mobile phone, without any kind of alarm system to alert people to his distress, her father had simply been lucky. He had fallen close enough to the telephone table that he was able to pull it over and call for an ambulance himself. Even then, as best as they could tell, he had been lying there for a couple of hours before he had managed it.

It was the thought that had plagued her every day and night since. What if he hadn't been so lucky?

The doctors had explained to her that the quick response had been a good thing. That he would make a decent recovery because of it. He had explained the terrible complications that could arise from a long delay. At the phrase 'dying bone' she had made her decision. She

18

had no choice. It was time to come home, whether she wanted to or not.

Which was why she was doing this job she now hated in the first place.

'Earth to Joanna.' That was enough to snap her out of her reverie and back to her father. No one called her Joanna, apart from to get her attention. Or to give her a telling off.

'What?'

'You were miles away. Are you sure you're okay?'

'It's just work.'

'Give it a chance. It's only been a couple of weeks. All jobs feel horrible for the first month or so.'

'I hope not. I'd like the horrible to be over with sooner than that.'

'In that case, think of the money.' He gave her a wicked grin and she smiled. She was, indeed, thinking of the money. Her home town now was powered by tourism, not much more. Jobs outside the industry were few and far between. The council had seemed like the best option. With that came a health and safety job she wangled her way into because of a stellar interview, a lightly fluffed CV that maybe over-stretched some of her previous experience in the area, and a complete lack of competition.

Now she knew why the competition had been so light on the ground. She had come to the realisation that her profession was second only to traffic wardens in the antagonistic response they provoked within the general public.

The money was good and it meant she could stay here and look after her father, without losing too much of her previous life. The mortgage on her own place still needed to be paid and the rent she was getting for it at the moment didn't quite break even. 'Well paid' was relative. Being the official destroyer of hopes and dreams might be well paid for the area, but it was certainly a step down from where she had been.

Official destroyer of hopes and dreams. She decided that sounded a better title anyway. It wasn't like she still had any friends here. When she walked through the streets, she could see how much things had changed. Or perhaps they hadn't changed, but she certainly had. Small town, small minds, small ambitions. That was how it felt.

She was never getting laid again.

'So what happened today that's put you in this mood?' Her father raised his tea cup without the merest hint of a tremor. His top half was still good. Still him.

'Site visit.'

'I would have thought that would be nice. Get you out of the office a bit. Into the fresh air.'

'That's what I thought until I got there.'

'Oh?'

'Let's just say, I had to do something that made me a bit unpopular.'

'I'm sorry Love. I hate to say it, but I think that's going to be a part of the job. Nobody likes to be unpopular, but it's not like you're being nasty out of choice. You're just doing your work.'

'I know. That's what I told myself.'

'Doesn't feel like it?'

'Not this time of year. Everyone wants to be happy and looking forward to Christmas. I turn up and they look at me like I'm here to ruin it with red tape and legislation.'

'It's not like that, I'm sure.'

'Even I feel like it is. If I feel that way, then I can't really expect anyone else to feel any differently about me, can I?'

'People always try to push their luck remember. All you are doing is protecting them from themselves.' He stopped and looked pleased with himself for the spin he was putting on it. 'Defender of the people? Protector of children from the...' he ran out of steam.

'Christmas tree?'

'Why do children need protecting from a Christmas

tree?'

'Far too many reasons than I would like. It would have been fine, I'm sure of it.'

'Then why did you have to do something?'

'A complaint from a member of the public.' That was it really. She hadn't exactly gone looking for trouble, although the woman who owned the bookstore clearly felt differently about the matter. The way she had looked at her, the comments. It was as though she thought Jo had gone there out of some personal vendetta, when nothing could be further from the truth. It had been a moaning member of the public with a specific enough complaint that she'd had no choice but to go and investigate.

It wasn't her fault that when she got there she discovered there were actual problems. The display looked so perfect too, in its haphazard kind of way. It really did feel like Christmas. The old fashioned kind, and it was possibly the first thing that had made her smile in the six weeks she had been back. Not that she could share the smile. Or show any kind of positivity, given the number of things that were wrong with it. The electrical issues were just too much for her to overlook.

Oh, she had been tempted. Really tempted.

She drained her cup of tea and resisted banging her head against the back of the chair too. She was still on probation. Overlooking something as serious as electrical code violations was enough to lose her the job. Her logical brain knew that.

Her less logical brain had been gawping at how gorgeous Kayleigh was from the moment she had stepped into the bookstore and had rendered her mouth mute for about thirty seconds. Even after she had regained most of her faculties, she had been unable to come up with any long sentences. Sticking to the point seemed like a much safer alternative than dissolving into a giggling schoolgirl.

Of course, shutting down half of her bookstore was not the grand gesture to begin a new romance with. In fact, it was the exact kind of act that Jo was sure ruined your chances forever.

She had seen the look on Kayleigh's face when she had told her the news. Everything she tried to do to make it better had been rejected outright. Jo had looked at the work calendar. Any new inspections were already booked up until the end of January. They were a small department and underfunded. The vague possibility of a re-inspection before Christmas had come out of a desperate attempt to win the woman over. It would have to come out of her own time, but as she handed her card over, she had been more than willing to offer a few of her free hours if it meant she could reverse the damage her visit had caused and put a smile back on Kayleigh's face.

Jo wanted to slap herself. She had no idea who this woman was, but she had been utterly mesmerised by her. Impractical crushes were kind of her thing. Which, when you lived in a big city, was fine. There was always someone new to move onto after you had thoroughly broken your own heart. A small town like this?

The suffering would probably never end.

CHAPTER THREE

Kayleigh stared blindly at the form on the counter in front of her as she stirred the pasta sauce. She had assumed that once the anger had died down, her brain would come up with a solution. The only problem was that she remained as furious now as she had been the moment Jo had walked out of the bookshop.

The sauce, something she claimed was a family recipe but was, in fact, straight from a jar but with a single extra herb thrown in, spat at her hand. She pulled it away from the saucepan and sucked the offending splatter from her finger. 'Tidy that up now please. Dinner is nearly ready.'

'But—'

'No buts. Now, please.' She followed the order with a stern look at the little girl sitting at the dining table. Kayleigh's cottage wasn't big enough to allow for a playroom, so the dining table was currently doing double duty as a six-year-old's arts studio. A six-year-old who was now staring back at her with disappointment. Emily understood the request to clear the table wasn't just to make way for dinner. After dinner, there would be no more colouring time.

Kayleigh knew she was lucky. There could be more defiance at this age. Instead, Emily was sweet and cheerful most of the time. Besides, that look of sadness and disappointment always got to her more. It was a significantly more powerful weapon in the war of child versus adult. Kayleigh caved. After the day she'd had, she couldn't stand for another person – especially a tiny one — to feel as badly as she did. 'Emily, if you tidy that up straight away like a good girl, I promise you can have another half an hour later while I tidy up. But only if you eat all of your dinner. Deal?'

Emily's only response was to beam at her and begin

shuffling the paper towards the end of the table. It had been her parent's old table, designed for a family. Parts were stained from colourings of her own, going back twenty years or more. Now, only the two of them ever sat at it. That left plenty of room for toys and craft materials to take up the other end. Kayleigh didn't mind the mess. It felt better to be annoyed by the clutter everywhere than acutely aware of the loneliness that expanse of oak could give her.

Kayleigh served up two helpings and carried them over to the table. She put them down and eyed Emily's clothing suspiciously. The pale colours didn't bode well. A few weeks earlier, Emily had declared that she no longer wanted her spaghetti cut up for her. Instead, she wanted to spin it around her fork too. Kayleigh had made a promise to herself long ago to celebrate any request for independence that Emily had, and this seemed to fall into the category. What had followed since was a very messy process of trial and error, but she was starting to get the hang of it. Not quite enough to sit through the meal without liberal protection from napkins though.

By the time Kayleigh had finished the surface and people protection project and they both looked like leftovers from a bad Halloween ghost group, dinner was cool enough for Emily to begin. Kayleigh took her first mouthful and forced it down. The encounter that afternoon had left her feeling more nauseous than hungry. The same could not be said for Emily, who already had more sauce on her face than in her mouth, but she had dived into the process with gusto. 'How was school?'

'It was okay. Mrs Brinkmore made us do spelling. She said we had to do spelling first.'

'Before what?'

'Before we could practice the play.'

'The Christmas play?'

'Yes. I'm a sheep.'

'I know you are. I bet you are the best sheep.'

'No. Mozzi is the best sheep.' Mozzi was Emily's best friend at school. Kayleigh doubted that Mozzi was the little girl's real name, but she had never heard her called anything else. She was just Mozzi to everyone. The two of them were inseparable, but with more than a little hero worship on Emily's part.

'I'm sure you are just as good a sheep as Mozzi is. Oops, be careful.' An inexpert flick of the fork and sauce arced gracefully into the air and over the table. 'Concentrate.'

'Mozzi is a better sheep because sheep jump high.' A statement of fact. Kayleigh watched carefully for signs of sadness or envy. If there were any, Emily was keeping them to herself.

'Sheep jump a little bit. I wouldn't worry about it too much. Next year, you'll be in another class and you will get to be something else.'

'I like being a sheep.'

'Oh. Okay.' Acting ambitions apparently were yet to take hold. That was good. Kayleigh didn't need a little drama queen on her hands.

She smiled and watched, not really listening, as Emily filled her in on the rest of her day. Kayleigh had never thought she would become an expert in this, the ability to half listen and nod in the right places. To capture the important parts in amongst the general chatter and ask the right questions. Being a parent was never her goal. Yet here she was. The two of them were doing alright, all things considered. She resolved not to let the problem with the health and safety woman ruin Christmas for them. It was a huge part of her life now, but that didn't mean it was more important than Emily. 'Come on, help me carry these plates into the kitchen.'

'Does that mean I can finish my picture?'

'Yes.'

'Okay.' Emily gathered the plate carefully and grinned. Kayleigh could see she was getting tired, but the promise had been made. It took a lot for Kayleigh to go back on her word, especially with Emily. The little girl was her whole world.

Kayleigh frowned. Her whole world was limping a little bit again. 'Is your leg hurting?'

'Yes.'

'Why didn't you say something?' Kayleigh put the plate down as Emily shrugged in response. 'Give me your plate and let's go take a look.'

Kayleigh deposited the second plate on top of the first and followed Emily through to the lounge, watching her every step from behind. Yes, there was a definite limp going on there. She kept an eye on Emily's changing height and general growth, but it was hard to notice the changes in someone when they were so slight and you saw them every day.

Emily sat down and looked up expectantly. 'You take it off.'

'No honey, you take it off.' Kayleigh stood firm on this one. Most of the time, Emily handled her prosthesis well, but at the end of the day, when tiredness set in, she tended to revert back to those times when Kayleigh did it for her. With a sigh she gave in and doffed the prosthesis, pulling it free from the limb that ended just above where her right knee used to be. 'Does that feel better?' A nod.

Kayleigh dropped to her knees to take a look. There was a patch of redness where it had clearly been rubbing. 'I think we're going to have to put some cream on this tonight. Then perhaps tomorrow you could use your wheelchair for school to give your leg a rest. How about that?'

'Sheep don't use wheelchairs.'

'I…' What could she say in response to that? Deny it? Kayleigh's brain scrabbled for some kind of reasoning. 'You could pretend you are a robot sheep for a day?' It was weak and she knew it. The look of bemusement on Emily's face told her it was not a winning argument. 'Let's see how it is in the morning then. Come on, let's go to bed.'

'But you promised colouring.'

'Are you sure you wouldn't rather just go to sleep and try to get better?'

'No. I want to colour.' Emily picked up her leg, ready to do battle on the matter if she had to.

'Okay, okay. But let me get your chair. Leave that there and I'll clean it for tomorrow.'

Kayleigh went into the other room to get the wheelchair. She needed to keep an eye on Emily's leg. Past experience had taught her that getting an appointment over Christmas when resources were stretched was no easy matter. If Emily was outgrowing her prosthesis, then the sooner they got it fixed the better. She was determined that Emily would have to use the wheelchair as little as possible, but without feeling ashamed of it. It was a fine line to walk. She wanted her to have convenience and freedom, but she had to be comfortable as well.

Nothing ever prepared you for this.

Twenty minutes of colouring later and Kayleigh could see Emily's eyes were starting to droop. It was nearly seven o'clock and they still needed to go through the bedtime routine. In addition to making sure teeth were properly cleaned (they usually weren't) and a story, there was a massage and some cream to now administer. Emily was a bright girl and her reading was improving in leaps and bounds, as was to be expected when owning a bookshop was in the family genes. Kayleigh was desperately looking forward to that day when she could get Emily to read to her whilst she did the other jobs, cutting the bedtime routine in half.

She was just being practical. Life had taught her, above all else, to just get on with it.

As Emily chatted on, slower now and slightly more rambling, Kayleigh thought back to the Christmas display. As she rubbed the ointment on sore skin, she was reminded of how important it really was. Something that the health and safety woman either didn't know or didn't care about. This would be the third year she had made the display big and bold and more than just part of a sales routine. In that final week before Christmas, the fundraising would begin in earnest.

It wasn't much, but the satisfaction and joy she felt each January when she presented the cash to the children's disability charity that had helped Emily so much was overwhelming. In the darkest of days right at the start, it had given her a focus and a meaning to keep going. Something beyond Emily.

Emily was her whole world now. But she had been someone else's whole world once.

Kayleigh swallowed, trying not to let the tears fall. Damn, this time of year made her too emotional. With the anniversary of the crash fast approaching, every day threatened to pull her into a black hole that she couldn't let Emily see.

'What's the matter Aunty Webby?'

'Nothing. I'm just tired.' A white lie. Apparently she wasn't as good at hiding the emotion as much as she had hoped. Only Emily called her Aunty Webby. Everyone else who knew the nickname had gone. Kayleigh's sister had taught Emily to say Aunty Webby right from the start and there had been no reason to change it. A stupid nickname because she had carried the book *Charlotte's Web* around with her everywhere for a whole year. Maybe longer. Her older sister Debra had started the name and had refused to let it go, even through those teenage years when the two of them fought all the time. How many times had Kayleigh threatened to punch her if she dared call her that again? Too many to remember. Now she would give anything just to hear her sister say it one more time.

Emily's hand slid out from under the duvet and into hers. Old beyond her years sometimes, she had been through the worst of the pain when she was too young to really remember it. But at times like these, when Kayleigh let her guard slip and her adult emotions show, Emily seemed to have a quiet compassion well beyond her years. Kayleigh cleared her throat. 'Right, let's read you a story young lady and then straight to sleep.'

'Read *Goldilocks and the Three Bears*.'

'Again? Really?'

'Pleeeeeeeease.'

'Emily, you have to be bored of that one by now.' Without waiting for a response, knowing that the answer would remain the same, she stood up and walked over to the small bookcase opposite the bed. As she bent down to choose the book from the top shelf, her eyes settled for a few seconds on the picture in front of her. It was the last picture she had of the three of them before Debra and Jack had slid off the road. A freak accident, that was what they said, but she wasn't sure she believed it. She had been fond of her brother-in-law, but never of his driving. He'd grown up in the town, a petrol head when he was a young man, whereas she had only ever known the sedate village. Life moved at a pace here where going over the speed limit never seemed necessary. Very few things could ever be that urgent. It suited her personality and it was one of the reasons why she had stayed when so many of her classmates had left.

But it had taken her a long time to stop blaming Jack for killing her sister and leaving her world turned upside down.

For the first year, whenever she broke down, it had been so easy to silently curse up to the heavens at him. Emily cried so many times during that first six months, not really understanding why her parents never came home. Not understanding why they didn't come to her in the hospital when she was in so much pain. As much as she had loved her Aunty Webby, in the beginning she had been a poor substitute for her actual parents.

The nurses told her things would get better. That kids

were resilient. She hadn't believed it. Then, at some point in the following summer, not much more than six months after they were gone, Emily seemed to adapt, just like the nurses said she would. It coincided, Kayleigh realised now, with the reduction in her pain. Her young body recovered from the amputation; she no longer looked down at herself with the quizzical look of someone who remembers something was there once, but can't quite remember what.

The child described as a Christmas miracle bloomed into summer in a way that made Kayleigh's heart melt. The two of them had settled into a life together, both accepting their fate. The journey had not been straightforward and the they had many lessons to learn that most people didn't, but they had tackled them together.

It was the photo atop the bookcase that they still said goodnight to every night. Kayleigh hadn't wanted to take her sister's place. She knew, with some sadness that had no name but was buried deep in her heart, that Emily didn't really remember her parents at all. They were the people in the picture frame and in the photos that Kayleigh made sure were around everywhere. They never aged and she would never remember their touch, unless perhaps in dreams. The day would come when she would be too old to be put to bed like this. When she stopped saying goodnight to them out loud. Kayleigh knew that when that day came, she would be the only one who could really picture her sister and still hear her voice.

Even so, for now, things didn't have to change. 'Goodnight Emily,' she said.

'Goodnight Aunty Webby.'

'Goodnight Mommy and Daddy.'

'Goodnight Mommy and Daddy.' Emily did a sleepy wave to the other side of the room.

'See you in the morning Sweetheart.' Kayleigh dropped a kiss on her head and turned the nightlight on. Emily slept through until morning most nights now, but Kayleigh was always afraid that she would try to get out of bed herself in the dark. Adept as she was, hopping around in the darkness was a sure-fire way to getting hurt.

As she walked back downstairs she checked her watch. Only 7:30. They had made good time this evening. Perhaps playing a sheep was more exhausting that she realised. Before she forgot, she went to the kitchen cupboards where she kept all the medicines and ointments high out of reach. There was still enough to nurse Emily through a bout of discomfort. No need to get another prescription filled.

At this time of year, even mundane tasks such as that had no place in her day. This year, especially, she had bigger fish to fry. With a cup of tea as a poor substitute for a glass of wine, she looked over the paperwork that the health and safety woman had left her. There, scribbled at the top, was her name: Jo Pearmain.

It didn't feel familiar. Kayleigh knew everyone in these parts, or at least that was how it seemed. The infuriating woman mustn't be local. Her accent had been somewhat indefinable — not that she'd actually said that many words to her. She had been too busy rummaging around on the floor, trying to ruin her life.

Any peace she had gained from a slow reading of Goldilocks evaporated in an instant. Damn, she was getting emotional. This was not the time of year to be messing her around. Without that charity, she would have been out of her depth from the moment she realised that Emily had somehow lived and was now her responsibility. Over the years, the volunteers had done wonders with Emily, but in those first six months, they had supported her just as much, if not more. There was a debt of thanks to a handful of the women she would never be able to repay. Instead, the yearly donation and push for visibility was the best she could do to show them her gratitude. There was no way this Jo Pearmain woman was going to take that away from her.

Resolution settled in her stomach and she grabbed her laptop. She checked the times of the local hardware store and made the decision to go straight there after dropping Emily off at school the next morning.

That was the easy part done. Finding an electrician who could do a — she checked the wording on the form — partial rewire at short notice was going to be hard enough. Finding one who wouldn't cost her an arm and a leg, no pun intended, would be virtually impossible.

CHAPTER FOUR

Despite being next to a window, Jo felt like her work desk never had enough light. She was sure that by the summer, she would be complaining about the glare of the sun on her screen, but for now it felt like she never really escaped the night.

At least she didn't have to go outside into the damp, grey mist. The alternative to site visits was all day sat at a desk, but she was happy to do the trade. Besides, the other woman who she shared an office with was having a day off to do her Christmas shopping, so for once she was able to sit in peace. The woman muttered to herself constantly while she jabbed the keyboard with two fingers, peering over her glasses after each completed word. At first it was fascinating to watch, but now it was just irritating as hell.

It was ostensibly a paperwork day. So far, she had drunk four cups of coffee to try to get warm and searched for Kayleigh Johnson on Facebook. She'd found a surprising number, but none of them had a profile picture that resembled the woman who had stuck in her head and refused to get out. The one she suspected was the actual Kayleigh Johnson she was crushing on had no profile picture uploaded, and the account was locked down. Who even did that these days? It was far too frustrating.

She tapped her chin, trying to come up with alternative solutions. It wasn't stalking, as such. It was part of the job. She was simply trying to make sure that Kayleigh wasn't a serial breaker of health and safety statutes. Or some other kind of criminal she need to be wary of.

God, it didn't sound in the least bit plausible.

With Facebook being a bust, she had no choice but to check out the plain old internet. She was about to type in the name again when she had a revelation. If Kayleigh was one of those people who protected their private life, she couldn't take the approach to her business. Business didn't thrive unless people knew about it. That much she remembered from her very basic economics classes at sixth form. She hit backspace until the search bar cleared, then typed 'Johnson's Bookstore Cotswolds'.

The ageing council internet seemed to take forever to return the search results. Coming back to this place really was like stepping back in time. Eventually, it loaded, with a variety of links. She scanned them quickly. Most of them were town level websites, designed to allow tourists to see what was on in the village so they could plan their day trip. Boring. Useless.

Jo took a sip of her coffee and went to page two, hoping it would contain something more interesting than the dates of the village summer fair four years ago. Didn't people think to update these things? A newspaper article link caught her eye and she reflexively clicked it. The headline took a moment to sink in. The picture, however, wasn't Kayleigh.

The mild jealousy she had felt the previous day when she had discovered that Kayleigh was the sole owner of a pretty little village bookstore evaporated as she read the words on the screen. She and her sister had run it together after their parents had died. They had been determined, according to the article, to keep the family business running as it always had done. Kayleigh looked at the picture again. Debra looked vaguely familiar. She hunted around in her ancient memories until she came up with the answer. Her first year of secondary school. Debra was the prefect who had kicked her out of the dinner hall once. It had seemed scary at the time, being shouted at by one of the big kids. Looking at the smiling face staring out of the picture, it seemed she hadn't been a dragon after all.

The picture was a family photo, but it didn't contain Kayleigh. Instead, a toddler was sandwiched between Debra and the man identified as Jack, her also dead husband.

Jo swallowed, uncertain about whether or not she wanted to continue. The little girl in the picture looked so happy. No outcome would be a good one.

She scanned back down the screen, finding the last sentence she had read, determined to continue despite the growing lump in her throat. A few weeks before Christmas, Debra and Jack had been killed in a car crash at a notorious danger point, known locally as Dead Man's Curve. Jo could picture it well. Many evenings before she had left for university, she and her friends had driven that stretch of road a little too quickly, drunk on the freedom that your first car and no sense of your own mortality can bring.

In winter, it lived up to its nickname at least once each year.

Heart in mouth, she read on, curious but dreading to know what had happened to the smiling little girl. The initial relief that she had survived became muted by the details. With no surviving relatives other than Kayleigh, she had been crushed in the crash, the car seat failing to protect limbs that fell outside its protective body. Doctors were working hard to save her arms but had already been forced to amputate one of her legs.

Poor kid. Losing your parents must be tough, but with that on top of it? She knew how much the loss of her own mother still stung and that had been as an adult six years earlier. Another reason she hadn't wanted to come back to this part of the world. Another reason why when her father had his fall, she felt she must. Life, in all its shapes and sizes, was a cruel thing to go through sometimes.

She hit the back button on the browser and continued skimming through the list of articles, feeling demoralised. Not only had she incurred the wrath of the most attractive woman she had seen since coming back from civilisation, that woman was turning out to be a saint. Given that Jo herself had effectively shut half of it down, she had clearly found the strength to keep going with the family business.

Speaking of which…

Jo clicked the link of a more recent article from the same local newspaper, a sinking feeling in her stomach. This one had the same smiling toddler, albeit slightly bigger now, in the centre of the picture, but this time it was most definitely Kayleigh with her, rather than her mother. Kayleigh was smiling too, but there was an indefinable sadness in her eyes. Those eyes were so expressive. The moment she had walked through the door, they had been her undoing.

She smacked herself on the forehead. She was a grown adult. This was not adult behaviour.

As her finger slowly scrolled the click wheel in the centre of her mouse, each rolling paragraph gave her a new level of self-loathing to sink to. The final part to the story had become clear. The child had managed to keep both her arms and now was bounding back to health in the loving care of her aunt. That, at least, was something to feel grateful for.

However, gratitude was not Jo's predominant feeling in that moment. Coffee going cold, she ran the full piece from headline (local woman raises £10,000 for children's charity) through the context (fun and amazing evening, with old-fashioned Christmas theme at its heart), to the final paragraph (so rewarding, she intended to set up the Christmas display in the store every year to raise money for this worthwhile cause).

Jo pushed the keyboard to the back of the desk then gently, repeatedly, banged her forehead against it.

Blowing her chances with women wasn't fun, but it wasn't exactly a new experience for her either. Being the Grinch who stole Christmas was. No wonder Kayleigh had been so furious with her. Jo had thought the woman was overreacting a bit, especially when she had done her best to keep the main bit of the business open. Jo had assumed that would be more important to her than some crappy Christmas sales technique.

Talk about being focused on the wrong thing. Why hadn't she said anything? Perhaps she had tried to. Jo had a vague feeling she'd cut her off more than once while her brain and mouth had been disconnected. She reached out and picked up her phone. Who cared if it was work time? She needed help. Selecting the number from her favourites, she pressed the button to dial and put the phone to her ear, before resuming her head on desk position.

'Hi you, everything okay?' The voice in her ear was as upbeat as ever.

'I'm an arse.'

'I can't hear you very well. You sound like your head is stuck inside a pair of boobs.' Jo sat up and looked at her phone. The woman on the other end was borderline crazy.

'A pair of boobs? Seriously Maddy, where do you come up with this stuff?'

'Ah, that's better. I can hear you now. So, no boobs?'

'Definitely no boobs.'

'So why are you an arse?'

'I thought you couldn't hear me?'

'I could hear you, I just wanted to make sure you weren't stuck in some bizarre situation where you felt you had to call me from inside someone's boobs with your dying breath.'

'I'm not dying and there are definitely no boobs.' The conversation with Maddy always turned to boobs at some point, but not usually this early. Jo, to this day, had no idea why they had ever tried dating. It had been a rocky and unsuccessful six weeks before they had decided to call it quits and just be friends. Of course, everyone says that when they're trying not to break someone else's heart. But life had continued to throw them into each other's path until, over time, they simply became the best of friends. It was much easier to forgive someone's maddening habits when you didn't have the sinking feeling of having to live with them for the rest of your life. 'But I've definitely been an arse.'

'This is about a woman though, right?' A five second deep whirring sound followed the question. Jo was used to the noise. Calling Maddy during the day usually meant she could talk, but there would always be power tools interrupting here and there.

'Yes.'

'I thought you said there were no women back in your childhood home? What happened to the barren wilderness?'

'I meant a lesbian barren wilderness. I'm not actually in the middle of nowhere.'

'Then come back here for a weekend. Don't go chasing straight girls Jo. You know where that always gets you.'

'I know, I know. Into trouble. But I've not even chased this one. I've just ruined her Christmas with my very existence.'

'Ruined her Christmas. I'd say that counts as more than being an arse. I'd say you've been a total—'

'Okay, okay, thanks for that. You don't even know what I've done.'

'Jo, I love Christmas. You know that more than anyone. If you've ruined her Christmas, then you're a terrible person, that's all I'm saying.'

'I rang you up so you would tell me I wasn't a terrible person.'

'You know me, ask me no questions and I'll tell you no lies.' Another whirr of a screw being drilled home. 'Ask me a question though and you'd better be prepared for the truth. So what did you do anyway?'

'There's this woman in town. She runs the local bookstore.'

'Chain or independent?' Maddy interrupted. 'I need the facts to picture this.'

'Independent.'

'Oh nice. This has all the makings of a Christmas Hollywood blockbuster. Have you had snow down there yet? You've got to have snow.'

'Shut up and listen. She owns this bookstore and I walk through the door and wham! She's gorgeous.'

'But straight? You made a move on her so terrible she won't recover before Christmas?'

'I don't know if she's straight. And my moves aren't that terrible.'

'If you say so honey. So you walk into the gorgeous woman's bookstore and what did you do? Set fire to the books?'

'I love the fact that I have a genuinely horrible scenario and yet you somehow seem able to come up with even worse. No, I didn't set fire to the books. I was there because of work.'

'Books are a health and safety risk now? I thought you'd be spending this time of year doing extensive cataloguing of uneven pavements.'

'This is the Cotswolds. There are so many cobbled streets that the council gave up on that long ago.'

'Why her store then?'

'Complaint from an anonymous member of the public about a Christmas tree she's got up in there.'

'People are so mean spirited.'

'I know. But once the complaint has been made, we have to look into it. Or rather, I had to look into it. I had no choice but to tell her she was violating a heap of things. I tried to do my best, but I've pretty much forced her to shut down half her store just before Christmas.'

'Wow, you are a Scrooge.'

'That's not even the worst part of it.'

'You took away her livelihood and then asked her out on a date? That does sound like your terrible technique.' The expletive filled reply got lost in another screw going firmly into place. 'But I'm sure it's not as bad as you say. It's not like you had a choice. Rules are rules.'

'I know. But I was looking online and—'

'Jo, we've had this conversation about Facebook

stalking before. You can't try to track down every pretty woman you come across.'

'Shut up. It was research. For work.'

'Suuuuuuuure.'

'Anyway,' Jo ploughed on regardless even though her cheeks were beginning to glow. Maddy knew her far too well. 'I couldn't find her on Facebook, so you're wrong about that. But I did find some articles online from the local newspaper.'

'Wow. Okay. Congratulations, you've sunk to a new stalker low.'

'Shut. Up. I need to get my confessions off my chest so you can make me feel better. I knew she was the sole owner of the bookstore and I admit to being a teeny, tiny bit jealous. But then I find out why. She'd inherited it with her sister and then her sister died in a car crash.'

'Damn that sucks.'

'I know. Leaving behind a kid. Kayleigh has been looking after her ever since.'

'Kayleigh? You're on first name terms with her already? That's not so bad.'

'I wish.'

'So she's a nice person. Please tell me you didn't hurt the kid?'

'Does that rank higher or lower than burning books in your scale of travesties I might have committed?'

'Tough call. Probably depends on the kid. Whiney or not?'

'I don't know, I've never met her.'

'Then why are we even talking about her? Come on Jo, if I was a priest I'd have kicked you out of the confessional by now. Get on with it.'

'The kid lost her leg in the crash.'

'Man, that sucks even more. Okay, hurting her would definitely be worse than burning books on the scale.'

'Good to know. Anyway, Kayleigh apparently raises money every year for a local disability charity.'

'She sounds like a nice lady. Far too good for you anyway. Cut your losses.'

'Don't you want to know how she raises the money?'

'Do I need to know?'

'With the Christmas display.'

'Makes sense. People are always more generous at the time of year. Spirit of giving and all that. Not to mention…oh. Wait. Didn't you say you had told her she had to get rid of that?'

'Yup.'

'You are a horrible person. You've ruined this woman's Christmas. And taken money away from lots of tiny disabled children. You should hate yourself.'

'And you are the worst friend ever. I told you that right at the start. You were meant to tell me it wasn't the case.'

'Jo, that's a pretty crappy thing to do to someone. But it's not like you had a choice.'

'I know.'

'I get it, I really do. Health and safety rules have nearly got me shut down on site more times than I can remember. But it's better than someone losing an arm or dying. I know you feel like an arse now, but what would you feel like if you'd ignored it and then someone got hurt? You'd feel pretty shitty. Not to mention losing your job. Or even ending up in jail. So yes, I'm sure this hot, probably straight, and out of your league anyway woman thinks you're an arse, but you probably did her a favour in the long run.'

'I think I liked it better when you were being mean to me. Not that I can really tell the difference.'

'If you want dating and sex advice, you come to me. For everything else, you're probably better off going to someone else. Seriously, don't beat yourself up over this. There was nothing else that you could do.'

'I need to make her see that.'

'Look, I get that you're going to have doubts about your new job and everything. Hold on.' Another drilling sound, this was significantly longer. Then Maddy continued without any further explanation. 'I mean, it's not like it's your dream job or anything. But think of how many we looked at online. You want to be able to live with your dad? Then this is the job you need to have.'

'I thought you were all about following your passion?' Maddy was the kind of woman who lived completely in the moment, whether that was when it came to her job or her women.

'Right now, your passion is looking after your dad. Besides, from everything you've said about her, you're not going to win her over. You just want her to see that you're not a terrible person so she'll date you.'

'Is there something wrong with that?'

'Faulty logic. You might be a nice person, but that doesn't guarantee she'll want to date you.'

'Now you really are just being mean.'

'Maybe. But you need to snap out of it. This job is going to make you do things you don't like all the time. That's life kiddo. Now stop stalking her on Facebook and get some work done. I want you to be able to sneak away early one night and come back here for a Christmas drink or five. We all miss you.'

'I miss you guys too. It feels like being banished to the wilderness out here.'

'How is he doing?'

'It's slow. I don't think he's ever going to be quite the man he was. He's hit a limit on how much he can do now. Physically at least. Mentally he's still the same funny old bastard he always was.'

'That's good. Focus on that. I gotta go. I'm getting funny looks from the boss.'

'Yeah, I should probably get some actual work done as well. Thanks for listening.'

'Hey, what are friends for?'

'Well, usually they give some sympathy as well, but with you, I'll settle for listening. Take care.'

'Catch you later.' The phone went dead and Jo looked at it for a few seconds before putting it down on the desk. Maddy had been right of course. A lot of the guilt had originally come from ruining her chances with the only attractive woman she had met since she came back. But now, the guilt was much, much worse. A real solid thing that felt like lead on her shoulders.

She put her forehead back on the desk and resumed the gentle banging of frustration. The paperwork could wait for another five minutes.

CHAPTER FIVE

Kayleigh called it the two-thirty slump. In the same way as carbs, there was a sudden descent into apathy that came at the same time each day for her book trade. Too soon for parents to be passing on their way to get the kids from school, too late for the morning tourist trade who were now all sitting down to lunch.

Some days, she relished that quiet time. When it had been an especially busy morning, it gave her a chance to get out from behind the cash register and walk the shelves. People were generally well behaved, but after a few hundred hands working their way over the same set of books, the displays started to look tired and out of shape. For some reason that completely escaped her, the autobiography of a reality TV fishing star was a hit this year, and her first task had been to restock in advance of the afternoon rush. She didn't know what confused her more; that there was even such a thing as a reality fishing show, or that this one particular individual had captured the hearts and minds of the general public. The one thing she did know for sure was that the book was an autobiography in the very loosest sense of the word. Industry gossip was that he had only the faintest grasp of the English language in its non-colloquial form and that they'd churned through four ghost writers before one of them could pull something vaguely publishable from the man's lips.

Taking advantage of the low footfall and in lieu of a proper lunch break, Kayleigh had unwrapped the cheese and ham sandwich she had made the night before and picked up the phone to Rob. More like a brother than a best friend these days, he answered after two rings. She needed someone to talk to and he was the only one who would listen and make the appropriate noises. 'It's only me,' she mumbled through a mouthful of cheese.

'Hello only you. Thank goodness you called. I was starting to go out of my mind.'

'You're going out of your mind? Wait until I tell you about my day yesterday.'

'Yes I'm going out of my mind. But please, feel free to make it about you. What's up?'

'Sorry, but when you hear, you'll understand.'

'That's okay, I was only going to moan about being bored anyway. No one ever wants to get a mortgage this time of year. There are only so many times I can pretend to be sorting out the files so that I don't have to go back behind the counters and help there.' Rob was one of the few people in the village of her generation who had decided that this was the place they wanted to be. Leaving had never crossed his mind either, not even as an adult when things got slow. Instead, he was the most popular mortgage broker in town, having made his way up from behind the cashier's desk when he first left school. He had helped her with so many things over the years, especially when things had been tough in the shop. The inheritance from her parents hadn't been much, but Emily and Jack had both taken out significant life insurance policies before they had died. Tainted money, in some ways, but Kayleigh had a duty to make sure that the bulk of it went to Emily's care, somehow leaving enough behind that she would also emerge into the world of adulthood with as many choices still available to her as possible. Rob had been instrumental in making sure she did the very best with what she had.

'Let's just say, the Christmas spirit is not alive and well in here today.' She looked over at the display, the occasional glint of a decoration in virtual darkness. The warning sign and roped off area made it more suited to Halloween than its true purpose.

'Slow day?'

'It's more than that. The actual Grinch came in and stole Christmas yesterday.'

'Um? I'm not sure I know what you're talking about.'

'Some woman came in from the council and shut us down.'

'What? She closed the shop? Why?' The actual panic in Rob's voice came through loud and clear. He knew how much the bookstore meant to her. Not just in terms of livelihood either.

'No. Relax. Not the whole store. Just part of it.'

'Can you even close part of a shop?'

'Apparently so. Unfortunately, it's the bit with the Christmas display. No one is allowed to go near it and it's in total darkness.'

'Why, what did you do?'

'I have no idea. She just came in, intent on finding something to ruin my life.'

'Take a deep breath. That seems a bit extreme. I'm sure she didn't come in solely for that purpose.'

'Really? She'd got herself a clipboard and everything. All dressed up in a smart suit and one of those heavy winter wool coats that serious people wear.'

'Right.'

'I mean, she can't have been any older than me. In fact, I think she might even have been a few years younger. She looked it.'

'I'm not sure what—'

'And she was really cool and standoffish. Like she thought she was better than me because she worked for the council and I just run a really old bookstore. Not that she's necessarily any cleverer than me. A couple of times I asked her a question and you could see her brain try to start to work before her mouth began to move. I mean, do you know how hard it is to just keep your mouth shut when someone like that is ticking boxes?'

'Ticking boxes?'

'Yes. Ticking boxes. Every little tick another part of my life on hold until Christmas. I have spent my morning on the phone to just about everyone in a fifty mile radius and do you think I can get anyone to come out and fix the problem she's made for me?'

'Well, no. Mainly because you've told me more about this woman than the actual problem.'

'Can you blame me? She's the one who came in here yesterday. Sweeping through the door and destroying everything.'

'You make her sound more Evil Queen than Grinch, to be fair.'

'Why are you being so flippant about this?' Kayleigh looked at the shadowed outline of the tree again. It seemed to be mocking her. Just talking about Jo Pearmain was enough to get her blood pressure through the roof.

'I'm not being flippant. It's just that you haven't told me what the actual problem is and for some reason you seem to think that it's her.

'Well without her, there wouldn't be a problem.'

'How old was she again?'

'About my age.'

'What did she look like?'

'I don't know. A little bit taller than me. Brown hair, just below her shoulders. She looked dressed for the office, which is why I noticed her coming through the door. We don't get many people at that time of day come in dressed like that. Her accent was strange, like it might have been from round here once, but I couldn't really place it. Why?' Rob had begun to laugh on the other end of the line. She squinted with suspicion. 'Rob?'

'You know I love you. But you have to admit, you've gone through a bit of a dry spell of late.'

'A dry spell?' She knew what he meant, of course. But understanding the words and accepting the meaning behind them were two very different things. 'What on earth has that got to do with all of this?'

'You know what they say. There's a thin line between love and hate.'

'Are you kidding me?'

'Come on, listen to yourself. Something has happened that means you have half your shop closed down in the busiest run up to Christmas. Any normal person would be calling me in case one of my clients could do whatever it is you need doing. I say whatever it is because you haven't actually told me yet what that might be.'

'I was getting round to that.' Kayleigh swallowed. Whatever Rob was trying to say, he was wrong. So very, very wrong.

'Really, because all I heard was you going on and on about some strange woman who came into the bookshop yesterday and turned your life upside down.'

'You made that sound completely different to what actually happened and you know it.'

'Do I? You know there hasn't been anyone since—'

'Please Rob. Don't. Not today. This is serious.' Rob could be like a dog with a bone once he got an idea into his head. He had spent the past year trying to get her to dip her toe back into the dating world.

Which sounded like a nice idea. But she had no clue what the dating world actually was for her anymore.

She was too busy to be lonely. Not only did she say it, she believed it. Rob was the only person still in her life who would even raise the possibility that she was attracted to this woman. Which she most definitely wasn't. Not that she was in the closet. She'd just never really had the chance to come out of it with any kind of style. When something as significant as having Emily arrive in her life happened, then people tended to make that the focal point of her world. Not that she could complain. She had done exactly the same thing.

Rob had nursed her through her first real relationship break up. It had been a hugely rocky road for six months and the separation had come as a surprise to no one. Perhaps if Kayleigh had been braver, she would never have got herself involved with a woman she was so completely incompatible with in the first place. But she'd been attracted to her and for someone exploring their fledgling sexuality, that had made Kayleigh grateful enough to act on it. She'd thrown herself headlong into the new experience, never thinking to ask the right questions. Then it had all crashed and burned in a spectacular fashion, leaving her to nurse her wounds. When the time arrived that she could contemplate taking those first small steps back into the dating world, she had been blindsided by the death of her sister.

Being a surrogate parent to Emily was more important to her than having a woman to warm her bed at night. Rob knew that. So he was wrong. Completely wrong about this woman.

'Okay,' Rob said, his sigh deliberately audible in her ear. 'If you're determined not to admit that this woman seems to have got under your skin, then at least tell me what she did. If she stepped over the line, then perhaps we can do something about it.'

'Well, yes.' That Rob might have some kind of righteous indignation that Jo had done something illegal hadn't really crossed her mind. 'She said the display wasn't safe.'

'When I came in last week it looked the same as it did last year. Maybe one or two more things on it. Perhaps.'

'You noticed that handmade reindeer decoration from Mrs Cardwell too huh?'

'It was hard to miss, if I'm honest.'

'What could I say? She's joined the local craft club and it's giving her something to look forward to every week. She's not been the same since the death of her son.'

'I appreciate that everyone needs an outlet for their grief, but couldn't she have taken up baking instead? I'm glad you've told me it was a reindeer though. I mean, I'd assumed, but it was hard to be sure.'

'Stop it. She's lovely. If I'd said no it would have broken her heart.'

'I suppose. But I'm not sure that the council can close

down a Christmas display because the artwork isn't up to scratch?'

'I wish it was just the decorations that were the problem. I could fix that, even if it did mean offending one or two of the locals. There were a couple of problems really. I'd always just walked over and got any of the books myself if people came in for something in that section.'

'That makes sense. I thought it was all the old crap that no one wanted to read in the back there anyway.'

'Philistine. There are loads of great books back there. I can't help it if you have no taste in literature.'

'Me and everyone else who sets foot in the place. So I don't see what the problem is. You just have to be the one to have the tree fall on top of you.'

'The problem is that I've got no one who works here full time to tell people that they can't go there and get one of the books themselves. Which means if the store is busy, someone could go ahead and end up with a tree on top of them.'

'I suppose that does make sense.'

'I know. But you have no idea how shitty she made me feel when she warned me that a child could get seriously injured if it fell on them. As if I wouldn't know what that felt like. As if I wouldn't care if I was responsible for something like that happening.'

'Ouch. She didn't know Kay. She wouldn't have said something like that if she did. You said you didn't recognise her. She's probably from out of town, just being a bitch. No one gets that kind of job because they're a nice person. Like that cow who goes around the supermarket car park and actually slaps fines on people who are there for more than two hours. She got me again the other day.'

'You park on there for work sometimes. What do you expect?'

'I think those of us who have chosen to stay and contribute to village life rather than taking our many skills to the big city should get some kind of free pass.'

'She only does it once a month as a reminder. Haven't you noticed?'

'Does she? It feels like every week. Anyway, surely you can fix that problem? You were making it sound like an absolute nightmare. Bit of signage, perhaps a cordon, like they have on the red carpet? Doesn't seem like it's worth shutting half the shop down for.'

'And there may or may not be a small issue with the wiring,' she finished with a wince.

'Wait. What?'

'It's more Grandpa's fault than my own.'

'I loved the old bugger, but he's been dead for quite a while now. Are you telling me you have a poltergeist in the electrics?'

'I might as well have. He exploited a minor technicality years ago when he had the place redone.'

'That sounds dodgy. Did you know about it?'

'Perhaps?'

'That means yes. Seriously Kayleigh, why didn't you get this sorted?'

'It was on the to do list. It just kept getting dropped to the bottom. I didn't have time to close down half of the shop while it got done. Not with Emily. Thank goodness Ms Pearmain didn't come in when Emily was sitting down behind the counter with me. She'd probably do me for child labour then as well.'

'Oooh, she has a name.'

'Stop it. This isn't about her, remember?'

'If you say so. But the electrics thing sounds pretty serious. Do you know what you need to do to get it sorted?'

'Not really. I've been ringing around every spare moment this morning, but no one will actually tell me what has to be done, they just tell me they can't do it.'

'Not a single one?'

'Two have said they'd come and take a look, but then they started talking prices. They know I'm stuck for time if

I want to have any chance of having it back up and running before Christmas. The amount they both quoted without even asking for any real detail was enough to wipe out any funds raised for the centre. I wish I could take it out of my savings, but there isn't enough to cover something like that. Not when I know that in the New Year I would be able to get it done for half the price. Or perhaps even less.'

'Isn't having half the shop roped off going to hit the business?'

'Like you said, it is only one of the locals who would want something out of that section. Most of the people coming in are looking for gifts. The tourists want to buy something regional and festive. I've got all the big hitters out at the front when they come in through the door. Some people might comment on it, but I don't think the profits are going to be hit too badly.'

'I suppose that's a small mercy then.'

'It doesn't feel the same. I'm worried.'

'Worried?'

'At this time of year, it's having the bookstore feel special that gets me through. Raising the money for a charity that has done so much for us both gives me a reason to focus. I'm worried that without it, I'm just going to keep thinking about what happened.'

'Oh, Kayleigh, I wish I could help.'

'There's nothing you can do. It happened and there is nothing I can do to change the past and bring them back. I can't make Emily's leg magically reappear. I know that. But having something to focus on allowed me to forget sometimes how unfair life is.'

'Look, I'll ask around. Perhaps someone has a relative who will do it for you cash in hand.'

'I need to make sure this is all above board Rob. She's going to come back to do a re-inspection of the place and if she thinks it's still not up to code, then there is every chance she could shut the whole store down. I wouldn't be able to afford to pay for it twice.'

'True. If she's as big a bitch as you say she is, then she'll be looking out for any little thing to pull you up on. Is there any chance that you can get someone else to come back and take a look? There must be more than one person in her department, surely?'

'I could, but she warned me that the chances of anyone else coming out this side of Christmas were pretty slim. I suppose she's right about that.'

'True. After Christmas is the same as not getting it done at all. I'll see if we can find a little Christmas helper. I can't promise anything, but at least I can ask.'

'Thanks.' Kayleigh could hear the misery in her own voice. Venting to Rob about Jo had been cathartic, but once the anger was gone, it left a void. In the absence of other festive emotion, despondency had chosen to fill it.

'Chin up, okay? We'll find a way to get this done. You fix the things you can and we'll find a way to do the rest. There must still be a few electricians in the area you can call?'

'I guess. There were a couple I left a voicemail for when they didn't answer.'

'Good. Ring them back. Just try not to sound too desperate. Money is tight for everyone this time of year and if they think they can cover the spending on their credit cards by taking advantage, then they will.'

'That's not very nice.'

'Human nature.'

'Cynic.'

'Yes, I am,' laughed Rob. 'I have no idea how you manage to stay so upbeat all the time.'

'I don't feel like I'm doing it very well at the moment.'

'You're doing better than most people would in your circumstances. I'll give you a call later. Let me know if you make any kind of progress.'

'I will.'

'And give Emily a great big hug for me. She promised

to show me her sheep impression next time I saw her.'

'Oh, she's been practicing hard.'

'To be that age again. When your whole world revolves around how well you can stay perfectly still in ridiculous costume and baa at the same time as everyone else.'

'Please don't undermine my niece's acting debut,' Kayleigh laughed, relieved to end the conversation on a lighter note. 'I'll talk to you later.'

As she hung up the phone, the doorbell tinkled. Somehow, the two of them had passed twenty minutes discussing the nightmare that was Jo Pearmain, health and safety destroyer of happiness. The afternoon rush would begin in earnest now, starting with the parents of young children coming back from school and then building up until it was time to close. She was glad of the distraction. Despite her promises to Rob, she didn't have the emotional strength to begin ringing contractors only to be rejected again. No, it was better to focus on what she was good at and count down the time until Emily came back from school, bringing her ever-present joy with her.

CHAPTER SIX

Jo swallowed, determined to get her racing heart under control before she took another step. Across the road, the lights of Johnson's Bookstore were soft and inviting, but she knew the woman who waited inside was probably anything but. To everyone else maybe, but not to her.

For a second, she contemplated simply turning around and walking away. After all, she had no good reason to be there. It was just a normal Saturday before Christmas and her only connection to the store was through work. She should have listened to Maddy when she had warned her to leave it alone. She certainly shouldn't have allowed herself to continue stalking Kayleigh Johnson online, refining her search words and social media platforms until she built up an image of the woman that confirmed what Maddy had told her from the start: out of her league.

This was a woman who had sacrificed her own life to bring up her dead sister's child. Alone. Jo didn't think it was possible to do anything nobler. But then Kayleigh had to go and be the good citizen of the village and devote her time and energy to raising money for charity. She made Jo feel like she had wasted her entire adult life doing nothing but partying and having terrible — but fun — relationships.

Now she had to grow up herself, of course, but that didn't seem to be quite the same.

So, in the space of forty-eight hours, she had developed enough of a crush on the woman that she had found herself volunteering to go into town for her father on her day off. His request had been a small one and certainly one that could have waited for another day, but she had seized on the opportunity so quickly he had looked at her with undisguised suspicion. Only the desperate would try to negotiate the sparse parking at this time of year. A fact which she had been reminded of only a few minutes earlier when she had nearly collided with an old woman who reversed out of her parking space with blind obliviousness.

She swallowed again. Her feet were frozen to the spot. When she had visited the first time, she hadn't really paid that much attention to the front of the store. It had been nearly dark and the weather had been miserable. Her only goal had been to get in and get out again as quickly as possible so she could be done for the day. This time, there was no rush. She could see the outside of the store and feel the tug of childhood nostalgia. She did her shopping online these days when it came to buying any kind of gift. Half the price and twenty times the convenience. For the first time, she felt a pang of guilt at the true cost of that. The shops on the high street were aimed at tourists now, not locals. They weren't really self-sustaining businesses in the traditional sense any more. It must be a struggle to survive.

As she forced her feet to move, her body was crossing the street before she was truly ready for her brain to catch up. As she pushed back the door and heard the soft tinkling bell above her, she realised that Kayleigh might not actually work in the store at weekends. She had a child to look after and everyone deserved to have some days off. Jo wasn't sure if she felt disappointed or relieved at the prospect. She closed the door behind her, determined to keep as much of the store heat in as she could.

Music was playing softly in the background. Traditional carols, unobtrusive. The soft choir voices were soothing, nothing like the Christmas number ones of the past thirty years with their raucous, pop and rock beats. No, the music was in keeping with the rest of the bookstore. It was a perfect choice.

Her eyes scanned the shelves. She felt a smile begin to pull on her lips at the sight of the books, nestled in amongst tinsel and fairy lights. The mix of old and new created a sense of mystery and she almost reached out, expecting to find a magical book that would somehow take her to another world. It was like childhood romance and fantasy, kept alive between these four walls.

Jo's eyes moved to the back of the store and the sense of wonder cracked inside. The Christmas tree, replete with oversized and mismatched decorations, was set against the darkness. A hazardous no go area, stood apart from everything else. At least Kayleigh had followed her instructions. It had never crossed her mind that she might simply ignore her and go on with things in the hope she wouldn't get caught out. It was, in that moment, a relief. Jo wasn't sure if she would have the strength to do the right thing and confront her. More likely, she would simply retrace her steps and make a hasty retreat. Plausible deniability would have to take precedence over her desire to see Kayleigh again.

Speaking of…

Jo looked around the room, until a pair of steely eyes behind the cash register locked with hers. Had Kayleigh been watching her all this time? Jo cringed. Had she been wearing the expression of amazement on her face as clearly as she had felt it inside? If so, she must have looked anything but a sophisticated charmer and more like a child. That had not been her intention.

There was a moment of terrible indecision. Should she acknowledge the fact she had been spotted and walk over, or should she continue to peruse the shelves as if they had never met before and she had every right to be in the store? Panic flared as the seconds ticked by, the carols fading into the background as the blood rushed in her ears instead. Breathe, she reminded herself. Just act casual. What's the worst she can do? Throw you out on your ear?

Yes.

Jo took a step towards the counter, making her way past a display announcing that the latest reality TV star had confessed all in his new book. She had no idea what secret fishing confessions would be, but they sure as hell didn't sound that interesting to her. 'Um, hi,' she said when she was a few feet away from Kayleigh. It seemed like a safe enough distance.

'What do you want?' Ouch. So much for the polite hello and forgiveness she had hoped for. Not that she had really believed it would happen, but it was one of the things she had allowed herself to fantasise about in the many times she had practiced this moment in her mind.

'A book?' Her brain supplied the obvious, if not quite truthful, answer.

'Then you've come to the right place. Which one?'

'Um…' For some reason, Jo hadn't thought the reply through to the end of the obvious line of enquiry. She looked around the store, trying to remember anything at all. Her eyes caught sight of a Children's book display, bright colours standing aloft in cotton wool snow. It tugged on a memory. *'The Lion, The Witch and The Wardrobe.'*

'That's one of my favourites!' An excited disembodied voice rose up from behind the counter. Jo saw Kayleigh visibly flinch as a child's head appeared. 'Aunty Webby has read it to me loads of times.'

'Aunty Webby?' Jo was confused until she saw Kayleigh point at herself, obviously uncomfortable at the revelation. Jo could understand why. It did remove the fearsomeness somewhat. 'Oh right.'

'We have several copies. In the children's section. Obviously.'

'Obviously.'

'Have you read the other ones?' Emily asked, oblivious to the staring match taking place between this new customer and her aunt.

'Not for a long time. A very long time.'

'I'm not allowed to read some of the other ones yet. Aunty Webby says they get too scary.'

'I think she's probably right.' Jo gave her a smile. At least she should get some bonus points for backing

Kayleigh up on this one. The frosty exterior failed to melt. Not anywhere near enough points yet, it would appear.

'This is my niece, Emily.' Kayleigh reached down and placed a protective hand on the child's head. 'I'd love to let her talk to you some more, but I'm worried if she gives you too much information about our current stock, you'll try to do me for child labour violations as well as everything else.'

If there was any humour to her words, it failed to come through. Jo felt the stab of guilt and sorrow pierce her stomach. It would never matter what she did or said. Kayleigh would always blame her for being the one to make her life even more difficult than it already was. She wanted to explain, but reminded herself that actually, she was here on her day off. She was nothing more than a customer. Instead, her mouth flapped up and down, waiting for a response that didn't come out.

Emily, oblivious to both her aunt's words and the anger behind them, came out from behind the counter. 'I know where it is. Do you want me to show you? I sometimes get to look at the books if I am very, very careful with them.'

'I think you should probably check with—' Jo was cut off by Emily walking round the side of the counter and setting off anyway. Her eyes snapped down reflexively to the limp, the false leg apparent to anyone who knew. She looked back up at Kayleigh. Those eyes had become even colder, a challenge for her to say anything. Anything at all. Jo knew it wouldn't take much to make her snap and then there would be hell to pay. For all of them.

A small hand slipped into hers, giving a quick tug in the direction of the children's section. Jo followed, unable to do anything else. She gave a backward glance to Kayleigh who, to her credit, said nothing, despite looking as uncomfortable about the situation as she was. Emily chatted on completely without awareness of the drama she was creating in the lives of the adults. 'Here they are,' she declared, pointing at the shelves in front of her.

'Thank you very much for your help. You make a very good shopkeeper.'

'Sometimes I'm allowed to help clean the shelves.'

'Maybe I need to talk to your aunt about those child labour laws after all,' murmured Jo.

'I'm only allowed to read some of the books though and I always have to ask first.' It was a solemn declaration of her trustworthiness. 'I'm not allowed to look at the grown-up books.'

'That's a very good idea. They're not as fun as these anyway.'

'Do you like grown-up books?' Emily gave her a huge grin. Jo mentally catalogued her current kindle collection. Yes, most of them would certainly fall into the category of books for adults. She cleared her throat, paranoid that for some reason, Kayleigh would be able to read her mind.

'Yes. I like grown-up books too.'

'Maybe when I'm seven I can read some of the other ones.'

'I think seven might still be too young for grown-up books. How old are you now?'

'Six.'

'I see. Perhaps you should stick to letting your aunt read these kinds of books to you for a little while longer?'

'I suppose.' Emily looked at her expectantly and Jo realised that she hadn't actually picked a book up yet. She saw the one she wanted and plucked a copy out from where it was tightly packed with the others in the series. 'You need to pay for that now.'

'Don't worry, I have every intention of paying for it. I wouldn't want to make your aunt cross with me, would I?' Jo made sure she said it just loud enough that Kayleigh would be guaranteed to hear. She had hoped it would make the other woman crack even the tiniest smile, but the expression remained as stony as ever.

'She doesn't get cross very often. Only sometimes

when I don't want to do things and she says I have to.'

'You should always do what your aunt says. She probably knows what's best.'

'She is very nice,' Emily confirmed in a confidential whisper. She began to walk back to the counter and Jo obediently followed.

'Did you find everything you were looking for?' The crisp tone could cut the atmosphere in the room quicker than any knife. Brusque, to the point — it was more like being told off by your teacher than purchasing something from a willing vendor.

'Yes, thank you.' Jo placed the book on the counter and pulled out her credit card. It was clear that however she thought this moment might go, whatever hopes she had for reconciliation, she was completely wrong. Now she had a book she had no idea what to do with and another kick in the guts to make herself feel even worse. To top it off, Emily was still beaming at her like the two of them were new best friends.

'That's £6.99 please.'

'Sure.' Jo slid her card into the machine and waited for the ageing technology to connect. She leaned in and lowered her voice. 'Look, I'm really sorry.'

'The payment will go through shortly. Sometimes it takes a while to connect.'

'I mean it. I'm really sorry for…' her eyes slid to the dark area at the back of the store. The tree a giant soldier lost in a no man's land.

'The internet connection can be terrible at this time of year. Every shop in the village is having to process card payments.'

'Please. Just say you believe me when I say that I didn't mean it.'

'I don't know who you are or why you are here. But don't try and push this back onto me.' The sudden change from store owner to a woman who was apparently about to kill her happened so quickly Jo barely had chance to blink. 'If you feel bad, then you should. But you have to deal with it.'

'I do feel bad. I want you to know that. I came in to see if you'd had any luck getting things sorted. I can see that you've done some of the things I suggested already. That's good, right?'

'You think that's good? I've made one or two minor changes that have done little else other than to make everyone aware that there is some kind of problem with the display this year. Sure, they were things you told me I had to do, but do you see any lights on there? Do you? No? That's because it's impossible to get an electrician to a job that big at this time of year unless you are going to make it worth his while. It doesn't take a genius to work that out. But you are clearly as dim as you are mean.'

'Hold on a minute, that's a bit unfair.' Jo was thrown off her defence by the card reader finally connecting and asking her to enter her PIN number. She stabbed at the keypad, pressing the first button twice and having to cancel it. She couldn't do that as well as try and protect herself from Kayleigh's barbs.

'I don't care whether or not it is fair. You have ruined Christmas for us and then you have the audacity to come in here and act like nothing has happened. Like we're old friends or something. We're not and we never will be. You have no idea what you've done.'

'I had no choice.'

'I don't care whether you think that or not. You obviously think you did something wrong otherwise you wouldn't be in here now. So take your book and get the hell out.' The careful control gave way and for the last sentence, Kayleigh's voice rose from a whisper to a shout. Jo could feel all the eyes in the room turn to them. Most people were browsing, more to get out of the chaos of the other shops than with any intent to purchase a book. Now they had an added bit of drama to throw to the mix as well.

Jo looked down to where Emily was staring up at them both, eyes wide and mouth open. Apparently Aunty Webby didn't lose her temper very often and certainly not with customers. Jo found herself desperate to shrivel into a ball and sink through the floor to hide her shame. The last time she had been publicly berated in such a way had been outside a bar after a rather disastrous first date. The woman in question had been rather drunk. Kayleigh was stone cold sober and twice as mean.

As she opened her mouth to offer another line of defence, Jo thought better of it. Kayleigh was right, after all. She had taken something beautiful and special and ruined it. Even if she did it for the right reasons, that didn't mean the damage could be undone. No, it was better that she take her unwanted book and leave the shop without causing any more of a scene. 'Thanks for your help Emily. It was nice to meet you.'

Emily just nodded, the talkative child she had initially met still stunned by the outburst of her aunt for reasons that she had no chance of understanding. Jo picked up the book and headed for the door. As she walked by some of the displays, she saw people looking at her and felt a sense of shame she could not quite name. A shame that she knew she shouldn't be feeling, but somehow felt anyway.

She stepped outside, letting the cold winter breeze cool her burning cheeks. She had tried her best to make amends. To show Kayleigh that there was more to her as a person than just her job.

She wouldn't make the same mistake again.

CHAPTER SEVEN

The image of Emily, staring up at her open-mouthed, was still haunting Kayleigh days later. She'd been timid around her since, watching her carefully with worried eyes. She had tried to explain it, in the simplest terms, but the words always seemed to be wrong. How could she expect Emily to understand it when she couldn't understand it herself?

Kayleigh stamped her feet, trying to get the blood flowing to her toes. She looked down at Emily standing next to her. If she was suffering, then she wasn't going to show it. Tonight was a big night for them both, but in different ways.

When the flyer had come through the shop door announcing the evening of the annual Santa procession through the town, Kayleigh's heart had sunk. She had always known there was a chance that it would happen one day. That the big, fun, exciting event of the season would fall on the anniversary of the crash. Each year, she would build up to this day. Each year, she would get through and put on a brave face until Emily went to bed. Then, when Kayleigh could be absolutely certain that she was asleep, she would open a bottle of wine and allow herself to dissolve into tears. One night when she allowed herself to feel the acute loss that would never be replaced. It was a day to just make it through. A day to survive.

It was not a day to cheer and wave and get caught up in the crowds revelling in their careless happiness.

A tear threatened to fall and she pushed the thoughts back down. For now, they needed to be buried deep, safe in the place she kept them the rest of the year. Emily was the brightest six-year-old she knew and would pick up on her lack of enthusiasm if she wasn't careful. Better to fake the excitement, in the same way she could generate instant amazement at a drawing that could, quite frankly, be anything, just because Emily had handed it to her and expected that particular response. Kayleigh willed happy thoughts. It was easier said than done. 'Are you sure you're not too cold?' she asked Emily, reaching down to tug the zip of her coat up higher.

'I'm fine.' It was the petulant, weary tone of a child who has been asked the same question several times over and is determined to give the same response each time, regardless of whether or not it was true. They had almost had words before they left the shop. Kayleigh wanted her to use the wheelchair. Emily had insisted she would be perfectly fine standing up. The two of them had reached a stalemate. It seemed like all Kayleigh could do was fight with people these days.

Eventually, she had relented. If the worst happened and Emily needed to be carried, then she could still just about manage it for short distances. It wouldn't always be that way. Emily would have to learn to accept that sometimes using the chair was going to be the practical option, regardless of how she felt in the moment. Her balance wasn't too terrible, all things considered. But she was little and people were careless. The crowds would push and shove and it would be easy for her to fall in the shuffle. Then there would be tears and Kayleigh wasn't sure she could handle tears. Not today.

They would unleash the flood of her own.

It was still early. The rest of the village would make their way down here soon, once they'd eaten dinner and had chance to change from their work clothes into something warmer. For now, it was a strange mix of very keen locals and the tourists who remained after their day out to the winter majestic beauty of the Cotswolds. At night, with the streets lit by Christmas decorations, she could see how the village lived up to the marketing. During the day, when the second downpour had made her worry the whole event might be called off, it hadn't looked at all majestic. Still uncertain, the two of them had eaten sandwiches in the store rather than go home and risk not making it back again. For all her stubbornness, she knew Emily would be devastated if she missed it. Tomorrow, with only a handful of schooldays left, there would be little talk of anything else.

Kayleigh felt Emily lean into her — a small concession towards warmth — and hoped that didn't mean she was already flagging. The advantage of being early was that you got a prime spot, one she was reluctant to give away. She heard some children laughing farther up the street, and her heart warmed at the excitement in their voices as she looked up to see where they were. Instead, she caught sight of a familiar figure. One who she had been feeling increasingly guilty about assaulting with a verbal takedown a few days earlier.

Jo hadn't noticed her. She was leaning down to talk to an elderly gentleman in a wheelchair. The two of them were laughing and it looked like they were both new to the contraption. Jo was moving in a slightly zig-zag motion, unable to get used to the gentle undulation of the pavement that seemed determined to throw them off course. She remembered those first few months well. Emily hadn't had the weight of a full adult to make it harder, but that hadn't stopped her mentally cursing the chair several times a day while she got used to pushing it.

Kayleigh watched as they came to a stop again, Jo reaching down and placing a gloved hand on the old man's shoulder. Gone were the severe work clothes and in their place, she was wearing bright red and green gloves. Had she been wearing those when she visited the shop on Saturday? Kayleigh wasn't sure. She couldn't remember a thing about what Jo had been wearing. She had been too busy looking at her face so she could make sure her insults were landing home properly.

Since the day of the inspection, Jo had grown into a mythical figure. A nemesis. Okay, that might be overstating it, but a heartless cow wasn't. The woman pushing the wheelchair didn't seem that way. She had obviously arrived early to ensure her companion got a good spot.

The penny dropped that she must be local after all. Curious then, that Kayleigh had no recollection of her at all.

Jo was crossing the street and heading towards them. A panic stirred — she could hardly move Emily out of the way so they could avoid each other — but she had no desire to repeat their previous confrontation. She was certain Jo would feel the same. Sure enough, in the middle of the road, Jo finally looked up and saw her standing there. She temporarily faltered and Kayleigh wanted to yell at her to keep walking. Once the momentum slowed, it was sometimes hard to get going again. The middle of the road was never the best place to come to a standstill.

Before she could say anything, Jo recovered her composure and carried on, with no choice but to walk directly towards her. Any hope that the two of them would pass silently by was shattered when she felt Emily tug her sleeve and point. 'Look it's the lady from the shop. Who I helped. Do you remember?'

'How could I forget?' Kayleigh murmured, forcing something that wasn't quite a smile, but at least wasn't a grimace, onto her face. 'Hello,' she said tightly. Jo, to her credit, at least had the decency to look as uncomfortable as she felt.

'Hi.'

'Hi lady.' Emily waved.

'Her name is Jo,' corrected Kayleigh. It wasn't Emily's fault that the two of them hadn't been properly introduced the first time they met. She had been too annoyed and Emily had been too excited.

'Hi Jo,' Emily tried again, doubling her waving efforts.

'Hi Emily. This is my dad, Herbert. Dad, this is Kayleigh. She runs Johnson's books.'

'I know who she is.' The man in the wheelchair beamed at her. Of course he did. Everyone around here knew the horror story that was her life. 'Although she doesn't know me. I knew her father, back when he ran the place. I used to come here every year for the Wisden Cricketers' Almanac. That was back when I used to be able to play the game and not just watch it.'

'Oh.' That hadn't been what she was expecting. Kayleigh found herself slightly stunned by the average response to the conversation. When people realised who she was, there was more often than not a gentle tilt of the head and a soft sympathetic voice, even all the years on. Today, of all days, she was relieved.

'I have a wheelchair too,' said Emily apropos of nothing.

'Do you?'

'Yes. Because of this.' Emily thrust her leg forward at an odd angle. Through the thick winter trousers it wasn't possible to see the false limb, but the unnatural lack of bend made it obvious.

'Emily,' Kayleigh began to warn her but then stopped. It was a strange way to introduce yourself into a conversation, but she had made a promise to herself that Emily should never feel ashamed of her disability. It didn't seem right to stop her talking about it.

'Do you want to see?' Without waiting for an answer, she reached down and began to roll up her trousers. The hard plastic glinted in the festive street light. Kayleigh threw an apologetic glance at Jo, who dismissed it with a smile.

'Well that's something else,' said Herbert. His voice was filled with admiration, but whether it was because of the honesty or an attempt to give positive reinforcement, Kayleigh couldn't tell.

'Have you got one too? Is that why you get the chair?'

'No, I don't have one of those. But my leg is metal now inside at the top. That's why I get a chair.'

'Metal? Wow.' Emily looked at him in wide-eyed wonder, her own leg now completely forgotten. 'Like a superhero.' She was practically breathless with adoration and it was all Kayleigh could do to stop herself from laughing. Herbert puffed out his chest, playing along, and gave Emily a cheeky wink.

'Maybe I am. But you know that superheroes can never tell anyone their secret. So you'll have to pretend you don't know.' Wherever Jo got her mean spirit from, it certainly wasn't her father.

Kayleigh looked up to see that Jo was looking down at him with the same sparkle in her eyes. The two of them were clearly enchanted with Emily. Under normal circumstances, that was the kind of thing that made her heart swell with pride. She hadn't chosen to be a parent and knowing that Emily was doing okay was something she usually found comfort in. Instead, this time, she was more preoccupied with looking at Jo properly. Could she have been too hard on her?

Jo looked up and smiled at her. For a second, it was like there was no bad history between them. Instead, they were caught up in the moment of an old man and an innocent child bonding over bodily afflictions with good grace and joy. 'Are you here for the procession?' she asked, feeling dumb the moment the words left her mouth but unable to pull them back in time. Lame. What else would they be here for?

'Yes. I haven't been to one in years. Not since I was a teenager. Besides, I promised Dad. He's been getting cabin fever so I thought a trip out would do him wonders.'

'I'm in a wheelchair, not deaf. Don't talk about me like I'm not here.'

'Chance to forget you would be a fine thing,' Jo said, but there was no menace in her voice. If anything, there was a hint of guilt. It was a feeling Kayleigh knew so well in herself it was easy to spot in others. The silence stretched out between them and no matter how much she wracked her brains, she couldn't think of anything else to say. If they hadn't started off so badly, she would have invited Jo and Herbert to stand with them.

'Hey my two favourite girls,' a voice boomed behind her, making her jump. Rob threw his arms around her and planted a kiss on her cheek, before reaching down and lifting Emily up into a giant hug.

'Put me down,' she squirmed, trying to escape his grip as he blew raspberries on her.

'Leave her alone,' laughed Kayleigh.

'We should go,' said Jo. The twinkle in her eye had gone and she looked awkward.

'Sorry,' Rob finally put Emily down and turned to them both. 'Have I interrupted something?'

'No,' said Kayleigh hastily. How had she forgotten that Rob would be joining them? She had no idea of the etiquette. Was she supposed to introduce him? Them? How could she explain any of this without looking insane?

'This is Jo and her daddy Herbert,' Emily helpfully supplied, sparing her any further agony.

'Nice to meet you,' Rob extended a hand, first to Herbert and then to Jo. Kayleigh saw his eyes widen as the penny dropped and the name sounded familiar. 'I'm not sure I've seen you around here before Jo?' His voice dripped with innocence and Kayleigh had to stop herself from elbowing him in the ribs. Not that it would shut him up. She knew better than that after all these years.

'I've only recently moved back to the area. To help Dad out.'

'That's very nice of you. What do you do?'

'I work for the council.' Jo was starting to look uncomfortable now. If she suspected that this was some kind of trap, she wasn't going to be too far wrong. Kayleigh prayed for some kind of intervention.

'The council eh? That must be fascinating?'

'Not really.' Jo looked thoroughly confused by the sudden and enthusiastic line of questioning about her job.

'We should really be going.'

'Why don't you join us?'

'Rob,' Kayleigh growled a warning.

'Thank you for the offer, but I'd like to get Dad down to the end where it will be a bit less busy. I'm a learner driver,' Jo pointed to the wheelchair. 'It's safer for everyone's toes if I get down there before many more people arrive. It was nice to meet you. Hope you enjoy the procession Emily. Give Santa a big wave for me.'

'I will. Bye Jo. Bye Herbert.' Emily said his name as though she was in church and he was some kind of revered saint. Kayleigh watched her stare after the wheelchair as Jo moved them away through the crowd with profuse apologies. Emily tugged on her sleeve. 'Do you think he's really a superhero?'

'I don't know. Perhaps. But you heard him. If he is, then he has to keep it a secret like all superheroes do. Do you think you can do that?'

'Yes.'

'Good.'

'I feel like I've missed something.' Rob rubbed his hands together to ward off the cold. 'Why would he be a superhero?'

'Hip replacement at a guess,' she whispered, unwilling to shatter Emily's illusions just yet.

'That was her, wasn't it?'

'Stop it.'

'I knew it.'

'Rob, you never know anything. And I am going to pretend I don't know what you're talking about.'

'You know exactly what I'm talking about. No wonder you were getting so confused. She's cute. And definitely gay.'

'On that, you really have no idea. Being friends with me doesn't give you automatic gaydar.'

'No, but I could see the way she was looking at you and then how she looked at me when I turned up. She probably thinks I'm your boyfriend. You need to correct her.'

'I need to do nothing of the sort.'

'Come on. You haven't had a date for so long. The two of you look really cute together.'

'Can we not talk about my personal life in the middle of a very crowded street please?'

'There's nothing to talk about. That's the problem.' For that, he got the elbow in the ribs.

'Look, just because she's gay doesn't mean that we automatically have to date each other. Or even have anything remotely in common. Besides which, do I have to remind you that she is currently the biggest thorn in my side and ruiner of Christmas? Think of the children Rob. They're going to miss out on thousands of pounds because of her. That woman. No one else.'

'She didn't look like the monster you keep making her out to be. I bet she only did it because she didn't have a choice.'

'I can't believe you're defending her.'

'I'm not. But you admitted it yourself, the wiring problem in the store isn't exactly a small one. You can't expect her to turn a blind eye. Plus, have I mentioned that the two of you looked really cute together?'

'For the first time in my adult life, I can honestly say I can't wait for Santa to arrive. With any luck he'll distract you from this madness.'

'Okay, I'll stop. Especially tonight,' he gave her shoulder a squeeze. 'But you shouldn't deny yourself a chance at happiness Kayleigh. Life's too short. You of all people should know that.'

He was right of course, but that didn't stop a rogue tear escaping her eye. As it rolled a hot trail down her cold cheek he pulled her closer. She had Emily to look after. Her own happiness didn't even factor into the equation.

CHAPTER EIGHT

Jo knew she was fussing excessively over her father. She tucked the blanket in tighter around his legs, despite his insistence that it was fine where it was. Under normal circumstances, she would avoid causing him any kind of minor annoyance such as this, but he was a distraction from the conflicted feelings she had racing round her head.

'Stop fussing,' he slapped her hand away. 'I do not need you making me feel even more of an old man than I already am.'

'It's cold. I don't want you to leave it until it's too late and you can't get warm again.' It was a partial truth. After a cloudy, grey day, the rain had finished pouring and with it came unexpected clear skies. It was a perfect night for a village tradition, but it was colder than she could remember in years. Probably because she was more used to drinking in bars before the icy night air hit her. There was nothing like an alcohol body warmer to make you oblivious to life.

She was sure several of the tea houses stayed open later tonight in order to take advantage of the crowds. Swapping from their usual caffeinated beverages to mulled wine, she found herself craving a mug, ostensibly to keep herself warm, but really to cheer herself up and numb the rush of emotions.

'Your friend seemed nice.' It was a sly question, asked at the moment when she was reaching back down in front of him. She knew he wanted to gauge her reaction. Knowing it logically didn't stop her from tensing.

'She's not my friend.'

'Oh?' He left it hanging there as a question and when she didn't answer, decided not to let the matter go like she hoped he would. 'The two of you obviously know each other. Work?'

'Sort of.'

'I'm not sure what 'sort of' means.'

'How about it means that it's none of your business.'

'I knew it,' he smacked his knee in triumph.

'You don't know anything,' Jo muttered. She looked around for some kind of distraction — any kind of distraction — but saw nothing that would work as an adequate diversion for someone like him. Once he got an idea in his head then he followed it through.

'I know more than you think young lady. Come on, tell your old man. I can't believe you've secretly been seeing someone right there under my nose since you got back.'

'We are not seeing each other.' On that, Jo at least could be genuinely emphatic. 'Do you want me to go and find somewhere that sells mince pies? I could really eat a mince pie right now.'

'Don't you dare leave me here alone in this thing. And don't think you can distract me with the prospect of a mince pie either. Although, now you mention it, one or two might be nice.'

'See, I knew you'd want one. I won't be gone long.' Despite his protestations, she darted off, glad of her sensible boots against the slippery pavement. She had no intention of leaving him for long, but neither did she wish to discuss Kayleigh out on the street with him. Not before she'd had chance to process what had happened.

She spotted the tearoom she wanted and ducked into the doorway. A queue was already beginning to form that snaked its way from the counter around the room. It would only get worse as the night wore on. That would be her justification when she returned to face the wrath of her father. For good measure, she'd get them both some mulled wine as well. She was driving, so he'd have to finish hers off, but that might be even better for reducing him to a state of placated calm.

Jo was debating whether to have two mince pies each or get the special offer bag of six, when she felt a tap on her shoulder. She turned around, her heart pounding. Rob stood behind her, a friendly grin on his face. 'Hello again.'

'Hi,' she said, unsure of what was meant to happen next. She barely knew Kayleigh, let alone the man who was probably her boyfriend. The crushing sensation she'd had when he first appeared returned and Jo knew she needed to get this woman out of her head once and for all. What was it about her that was so fascinating anyway? It made no sense, but it was real enough to reduce her to a moment of sheer awkwardness with the man looking at her right now.

'I'm sorry if I made you feel uncomfortable back there,' he said. 'Kayleigh told me who you were.'

'Wow. I'm surprised you're still talking to me.'

'I'm not going to lie. You're not exactly her favourite person right now.'

'Thanks for reminding me. She's made it perfectly clear without your help though. So if you've come over here so you can tell me off as well, then please don't. I'm here with my father and he doesn't get out much these days. I understand that you're probably mad at me too. But I'm not at work now and I deserve to be able to spend time with my family as much as anyone else.'

'Whoa, take it easy. I wasn't going to have a go at you. I've known Kayleigh for a long time. Since we were in school. She's a lovely person.'

'I'm sure she is, but that doesn't mean I can change the facts.'

'I'm not asking you to. I understand that she's not exactly in the right here. But she's had a rocky road to get here.'

'I know.'

'I thought you might.' He pointed forward and she turned to see that the queue had moved. The two of them shuffled closer to the counter, but not close enough as far as Jo was concerned. She wanted this weird conversation to be over. 'I just wanted to say, when this all blows over, give her a chance.'

'I'm not sure I understand what you mean.'

'She's been lonely for a long time. Looking after Emily and that bookstore is all she does. She could use a friend. I don't know, I just thought the two of you looked like you could…' he trailed off, clearly unable to put what he was thinking into words. Jo had started the conversation apprehensive, but now she was just confused.

'I'm not sure that our paths are really likely to cross. I told her I'd come out and do a re-inspection before Christmas, but she's made it clear that she's not going to be able to get the work done in time.' Jo shrugged and the helplessness she had been feeling since that first day returned. 'So there's not a lot I can do.'

'Okay. But when all this blows over, if for some reason the two of you do end up bumping into each other, give her a chance. This time of year is the worst for her. She's strong for Emily and she puts all her spare energy into raising funds for that charity, but it's all to avoid having to deal with her grief. I'm her best friend, but there is only so much I can give her.'

'It must be hard for her.' Jo nodded, feeling genuine sympathy. Then the last sentence sunk in. He was her best friend? Just her best friend? Maddy's warnings rang clear in her head. The woman was both complicated and out of her league, even if that was what he was trying to put across. He gave her a giant grin. Yes, that was what he was trying to put across.

Something a little like hope flared in her chest. He didn't look like the matchmaking type. She bit her lip, unwilling to say something that would make her look like a fool or tip her hand. But she had to know. 'Her best friend? I assumed you were her boyfriend.' It was an innocent enough question when taken out of context but from his smile she could see he knew he had got her hook, line and sinker.

'Boyfriend? Good god no. She's more like a sister to

me. Dating her is the last thing I would ever do. Besides, I'm not really her type either.'

'Oh?'

'No. She's not dated anyone for years. But when she finally gets back on the horse, I think she'll be looking for, shall we say, a slightly more feminine touch than the one that I could give.'

'Oh,' said Jo again, this time with an awkward, nervous swallow that made the word come out as a squeak.

'What? Shit, have I totally misread the situation? I'm sorry, I just assumed...' It was amusing how the cocky confidence drained away in an instant. She let him flounder for a few seconds more before putting him out of his misery.

'No, you haven't misread the situation. Well, you have if you think she's going to forgive me any time this decade, but other than that, I know what you're saying.'

'Phew. I thought I was about to get a slap there for my matchmaking attempts.'

'I'm sure she will if she finds out. But genuinely, she's not interested in me. The only reason she didn't scream at me again this time was because my father and Emily were there. I think she upset Emily a bit last time.'

'Yes, it probably would. Kayleigh isn't one for anger. Or any kind of strong emotion these days really, unless you include the protectiveness she feels for Emily. You're the first person to get under her skin in a long time.'

'Sadly, it's not in a good way.' They had reached the front of the counter. Despite the strange elation buzzing in her head, she was also glad the conversation was over.

'Give her a chance,' he said over her shoulder, like a devil she didn't need to hear. 'If for some reason you do see her again under different circumstances, don't blow her off just because of this one incident.'

Jo ordered a bag of mince pies and two plastic cups of mulled wine. She tucked the bag under her arm and resisted the urge to drain the hot liquid in one go before she'd even left the shop. Instead, she hurried back to her father, Rob's words still buzzing in her ears.

The procession was on the move at the top of the street. Given the relative size of the village, Santa didn't move at great speed, otherwise the whole thing would be over with before people had chance to go back for the second round of mince pies and mulled wine. It might be a community building spirit, but Jo wasn't stupid enough to think that it wasn't motivated, in large part, by money.

'Those mince pies better be good,' he grumbled, taking one of the plastic cups from her. 'I told you not to leave me here on my own.'

'I'm sure you were fine.'

'I kept getting worried you hadn't put the brake on properly and I'd go rolling off down the hill.'

'Don't be silly. Here, have these.' She put the bag of mince pies down in his lap, wrapping her hands around the plastic cup. She took a sip, relieved to find it was surprisingly good. The warmth filled her belly and made her feel like she was glowing from the inside.

'I suppose they're not too bad,' her father said around a mouthful of pastry. 'Try one.'

Jo reached down and pulled one from the bag, feeling for the first time that Christmas was nearly here. Since she had returned, it had been work and her father's health that had filled her mind and her free hours. The festive season hadn't really taken hold once she'd been told she was the reason for ruining it. Now, as the crowds around them thickened and the air grew loud with chattering excitement, it felt like the holiday was really upon them.

'I haven't forgotten, you know,' he said, polishing off the mince pie with relish and washing it down with mulled wine. 'The legs might have gone, but my mind is still sharp enough to spot when someone is trying to distract me with food and drink.'

'I don't know what you're talking about.'

'Yes you do. You might as well tell me. I know we

weren't really involved with each other's lives. Not when you were away. And that's okay. Young people should grow up and live their lives their own way. Do what they want to do. Trust me, it goes by so fast. It doesn't seem five minutes since I was your age and now I'm here, sitting in this thing.'

'This is meant to be a happy occasion. You're starting to sound morbid.'

'I'm not saying I'm going to die, just that my dancing days are over, that's all. But you're living with me now and I don't think I've told you how much I appreciate that. I wish you didn't have to and I've told you not to, but I am glad that you're around.'

'I'm glad to be around.' Jo meant it too. It was a culture shock and yes, she missed her friends. But being with him had given her a different kind of joy and connection. One she was glad to have the chance to explore before it was too late.

'Good. So I don't want you to feel like you can't have any life because of me. Or that you can't tell me about your life either. I know I wasn't a great dad when you told me, you know, about what you were, but I want you to be happy. That's the main thing.'

'Thanks.' God, this was awkward. Jo shoved another mince pie in her mouth to give herself a reason not to have to talk.

'So, go on then.'

'Go on what?' her mouth was slightly over-stuffed and a crumb popped out, landing on his shoulder. She brushed it away before he noticed.

'Tell me about your friend.'

'Dad, I promise I wasn't lying when I said she wasn't my friend. The exact opposite.'

'Surely you haven't been back here long enough to make an enemy?'

'Yes, apparently I have. It wasn't really my fault. It was work.'

'Everyone has to work. You shouldn't feel bad about the fact.'

'Yes, I should. Did you know she does some kind of Christmas thing in the store each year to raise money for charity?'

'I think I've read about it in the paper. It's a good cause. That niece of hers is a brave little thing.'

'Yeah, well it probably won't be happening this year. I shut it down.'

'Oh.'

'See. Now you can see why she's not my friend. And before you tell me how terrible it is, there is nothing you can say that's worse than what I've already said to myself. I am a horrible person.'

'Jo, you are a lovely person. I'm not just saying that because you're my daughter. You are. This is just one thing that feels bad because it makes someone else unhappy. The fact you're as bothered about it as you are just means you are nice. Not the opposite. Another one?' he held a mince pie up and she took it from him. Might as well break the diet for Christmas already.

'Thanks. I just wish I could make it better. But I can't even do that, because I'm not allowed to show any kind of special treatment for anyone. Not even if it means that the charity would get its money.'

'No special treatment?'

'Professional boundaries. It's part of the job. I've already said I would come back and do an inspection if she got it done. I'd do it in my own time. That's bad enough but I reckon I'd be able to get away with it. But I want to be able to do more. I could do more, but my hands are tied.'

'Look around you. See all these people. See how happy they are? This is what life is about. Especially this time of year. Christmas is for good deeds. Miracles. That little girl we met back there? She's a miracle and it shines from her. If you can fix this mess, then you should.'

'Dad, that sounds like a lovely thing to say. But be realistic. What if doing it means I lose my job?'

'So?'

'What?' The mulled wine was either going to his head or hers.

'So what if you lose your job? It's just a job.'

'I hate to remind you of this, but it's a job that pays me money. Money I need to live on. To pay the bills. You know what it's like around here. A good job is hard to find. I was lucky enough to get this one in the first place. I can't throw it away. I need to be able to stay here with you.'

'Jo, it breaks my heart to think that you would feel that way. I've seen you this past week. You've not been yourself. Doing this has made you so unhappy. I know it's part of the job, but it's a job you wouldn't be doing if it wasn't for me. I don't want you to ever sacrifice your happiness for me like that. Or your integrity. I think you know the right thing to do.'

'Do you really think so?' His words made sense on the surface, but she wasn't sure he really understood the implications of what he was saying. If she got caught doing something so against the rules while she was still in her probationary period, then there wouldn't be a slap on the wrist. She wouldn't have to go through a mountain of HR paperwork and meetings so they could fire her. The desk would be emptied before she even had chance to think about it.

On the other hand, he was right. She had been unhappy. For Emily as much as Kayleigh, she had wanted to wave a magic wand and make it all better.

Perhaps it was the mulled wine. Perhaps, for the first time since she was a child, she was listening to her father's advice, rather than just rolling her eyes at the old man. She wiped her greasy fingers on her jeans and pulled the phone from her pocket. Before she could change her mind, she scrolled through her list of contacts and dialled. The jingling of bells from Santa's sleigh grew louder and she pressed the phone closer to her ear.

'Maddy? I need you to do me a massive favour.'

CHAPTER NINE

Kayleigh was emotionally and physically exhausted.

The anniversary of her sister's death was a day to keep busy, a day to wear herself out in the hope that sheer exhaustion would carry her through the tears and into a deep and dreamless sleep. This year, she had taken it to a whole new level.

She should really have double-checked the weather forecast that morning before she had got herself ready for work and Emily packed up ready for school. With Emily she was always overcautious regardless. With herself, not so much. The sudden changes in wind direction and the clear skies it brought with them had caused the temperature to plummet. At some point, Rob had noticed she was wracked with violent shivers and had given her his scarf to help. It had, for a little while, before the seeping cold had taken hold once more.

As she unlocked the front door and ushered a tired Emily inside, she thought back to his behaviour that evening. He had been true to his word and not mentioned Jo again. The two of them had known each other for so long he was an open book. In his silence, she noticed something else.

As she stripped off her boots and tried to squeeze life back into her freezing toes, she tried to work out the moment at which he went from playful to something slightly more devious. It was after he had gone to get the mince pies. He had returned looking smug in a way that pastry and alcohol alone could not achieve. Throughout the evening, he kept bumping her shoulder, like he was bursting with some strange secret that he knew and wanted to share but couldn't. It was annoying.

He hadn't even tried to convince her to have a glass of mulled wine. Not today. There was no way she would be getting behind the wheel with even the tiniest drop of alcohol in her system. Not that Jack had been over the limit when he crashed the car. But to even risk it, tonight of all nights, seemed to be tempting fate. He knew she felt that way, and instead had dutifully brought her a cup of tea with her food.

'Go and get ready for bed,' she called out to Emily, who was happily chatting away to herself now in the other room. The poor kid was so excited but Kayleigh had spotted her eyes closing on the drive home. It was way past her usual bedtime, but seeing Santa had got her too wired to sleep. It would take a good story tonight to get her to nod off and the morning would bring with it the consequences.

Kayleigh walked through to the kitchen. She paused for a second, the prospect of a glass of wine to take the edge off far more tempting than she would like it to be. No, that would have to wait. Another cup of tea was what she needed to make herself feel warm again. She opened the cupboard and looked at her selection. Chamomile was just what she needed. She hated the taste of it, but it did have a relaxing effect. She'd learned to get used to the initial unpleasantness over the years if it meant her shoulders moved a little lower than her earlobes.

As she waited for the kettle to boil, she noticed the council paperwork still sitting on the work surface. That afternoon, when passing trade began to pick up again as parents collected their children from school, Kayleigh had finally admitted defeat and turned her attention back to serving customers. She had rung every single person in the book and no one could do what she wanted in the right time or for the right price. She had done her best, but every single avenue had been exhausted. Even Rob had run out of people to ask.

A thud above made her freeze for a second, but then she heard Emily moving around and laughing. She breathed a sigh of relief, nursing the drink close to her chest. She was going to need every single ounce of calm it could offer at this rate.

She looked at the paperwork again, seeing where Jo's scrawl had signed the deal at the bottom of the page. The anger flared briefly, but was muted by the events of the evening. She was still livid, furious that the world would do this to her. But it was also hard to reconcile the box-ticking, red-tape-conforming council official who had been in her shop with the woman she had seen out on the streets tonight. There had been a real person underneath the sharp suit after all, it seemed. One that, for all the denial she had given Rob, was indeed an attractive woman. Her type, she supposed, if she thought about it too much. Could you have a type when you had only ever dated one woman before? Those were the kind of questions people would normally be asking before now. They'd not even crossed her mind for three years or more.

Jo's father had been a hoot too. Emily had continued talking about him throughout the evening. She didn't think she'd ever seen such a connection between a young and old soul happen so instantaneously before. But if it made the use of the wheelchair a more agreeable option when the circumstances dictated, then Kayleigh was more than happy for Emily to be won round by him. He must have been quite the charmer in his youth.

Could Jo be the same? She'd not really given her much chance to show it. If she would even be interested at all. She only had Rob's reassurances on that front and how much could you trust a man's opinion on that? Still, she thought there had been a connection there, of sorts, when her guard had been down. It was a shame that the two of them were unlikely to meet again. Or that she would be able to forgive her any time soon. Beneath the admission that the other woman was attractive, the anger still simmered at the consequences of her actions. It messed with her head, but it was unlikely she would be able to change the way she felt.

Gone were the days when life could be simple. Uncomplicated by responsibilities or the weight of her own fragile emotions. She hadn't even realised it at the time, but she sure as hell missed it now.

Another bump from upstairs and she realised she had allowed bedtime to be delayed for long enough already. Her ten minutes of peace came at a significant cost in the morning. She took another sip of tea and placed the mug down next to the paperwork. It would still be there when she got back, that bittersweet reminder.

Determined to be stern, she trudged up the stairs to Emily's bedroom. All fierceness dissolved at the sight of Emily in a state of strange undress, having apparently decided tonight was the night to mix-and-match her pyjamas. A pink and green ensemble that would either fail or be a massive success in the fashion world, depending on which year it was. It offended Kayleigh's eyes. 'What on earth are you doing?'

'I'm a superhero princess.' Emily sat on the bed with her hands on her hips, as if it was completely obvious.

'Right.'

'This is my princess part,' she pointed at the pink top, 'and this is my superhero part.' The green pyjamas were more leprechaun than superhero, but Kayleigh let it slide.

'Well, Little Miss Superhero Princess, I think it's time you went to sleep.'

'Story first.'

'Of course. What would you like? It has to be a short one. It's long past your bed time and there's still school tomorrow.'

'It's not proper lessons. Mozzi said so.'

'And I suppose you think Mozzi knows everything, don't you?'

'Yes.'

'Well, she doesn't always. So if I say you have to do something, then you have to do it, even if she says you don't have to.'

86

'But Mozzi—'

'No buts. Those are the rules. And tomorrow you have a play to practice. That will be hard work. I don't want my little sheep falling asleep on the stage.'

'I won't.' A slight quiver of the lower lip was a sure giveaway that Kayleigh was doing the right thing by sticking to her guns. Emily was overtired and all it would take was the slightest, most innocuous thing to tip her over into a full scale meltdown.

'Good. Can I check your leg before we read please?'

'Okay.' Emily presented it to her to look at. Each new pair of pyjamas went through the exact same process. Kayleigh waited until Emily went to bed and then cut down the right leg, making it the same length as her limb. Then she would painstakingly sew a new hem to make it look the same as the other one. The first time she had done it, several hours had gone by before she was satisfied with the result. It had still looked terrible; uneven and badly sewn. She had grown better over the years, doing it now without really thinking, watching a TV show at the same time.

The sore, slightly inflamed patch that she had spotted a week ago was now in a holding pattern. Slightly worse at the end of each day, but by the morning it had calmed down considerably. Kayleigh's fear was that after a night of stubbornness out in the cold, it would be back to where it had started. By some miracle, it didn't look any worse than normal. 'How does it feel? Sore? Itchy?'

'Okay,' Emily shrugged. That was good. As long as there was no pain, they could continue to manage it.

'Good. Now you think about which book you would like us to read while I just rub a bit of cream on it.' Kayleigh went to the bathroom to fetch the tube, hoping that Emily wouldn't choose anything too emotionally traumatic tonight. Until she had come into her care, Kayleigh hadn't realised how much sheer horror was buried in children's fairy tales. There was always evil lurking around every corner and, far too frequently for her taste, death. It was an area of discussion that always felt like she was skating on thin ice but tonight, with the ghost of her sister watching over them, it would be too much to handle.

She was relieved when she returned to the room and saw that Emily had already made her choice. It was an old book, battered around the edges from frequent use. But it was also short. That got bonus points. That Emily was silently mouthing along to the words as she turned the page was also a good sign. Not that she was reading them properly quite yet. But knowing them well enough to give the appearance of reading meant that she could make a start on her own while Kayleigh began to gentle massage her swollen limb. Despite Emily's reassurances, it felt hot to the touch. Kayleigh had to remind herself that it was completely normal. It was not a sign of septicaemia. There would be no midnight runs to the hospital tonight.

'Aunty Webby?'

'Yes Sweetheart.'

'When is Santa coming?'

'Next week. And only if you've been good remember.'

'Do you think he'll know how to find me?'

'I would imagine so.' Kayleigh paused in her massaging to look up. Emily's face was pulled into a tight little worried frown. 'Why do you think he wouldn't?'

'Because this is your house.'

'I'm too big for Santa to come to me. Don't worry, he won't be bringing me presents instead.'

'It's not that.' Emily frowned harder, as if that was the most stupid thing she had ever heard.

'Then what is it?'

'This is your house. But Mozzi said that Santa had our names on a list.'

'He does.'

'But you have a different last name to me. What if he can't find me?' The quiver that had been so obvious before now threatened to spill over. Such an innocent but genuine fear that felt like a stab to her chest.

'He knows everything Sweetheart. I promise you, he'll know where to find you.'

'But what if he doesn't?'

'He will.' Kayleigh moved up the bed to sit next to Emily, pulling her into her arms. From across the room, the light glinted on the picture frame, her sister's face smiling at them both. How could it even be? This time, three years ago, she had just heard the news. The clock had frozen for her that night. The night that had made the two of them into a little family of their own. Now the differences from a normal family were starting to make sense to Emily in a way they never had before.

Promises were useless, Kayleigh knew that. Even ones she would once have made with certainty. Fate could deal a single cruel blow at any moment it wished, leaving everyone stunned and dazed in its wake. 'I promise you, he has found you here every year since you came to live with me and he will this year too. It doesn't matter what our names are.'

'Maybe,' Emily stuttered through the tears she was trying to stop, 'maybe I should have the same last name as you now. Now that I live with you.'

Kayleigh's heart splintered into a thousand tiny pieces, each too small to ever be put back together properly again.

CHAPTER TEN

For the first few weeks after she moved back, Jo had found herself compelled to stay in the same room as her father each evening. No matter how tired she was, she had refused to go to bed until he was ready to do so himself. With good reason. For that first month, he was still going to sleep upstairs. Despite his need for the wheelchair most of the time, he could still technically walk. Which meant he could get himself upstairs and into the bedroom he had slept in for over forty years.

Theoretically.

The first time Jo had watched him make the journey, she thought the panic and fear would give her a heart attack. Each step was made with such extreme, slow deliberation that it reminded of her of a man nearing the summit of a mountain, body physically drained and oxygen levels low. Every few steps he wavered, unable to find his centre of gravity and she had been certain that it would be the moment when he toppled backwards completely. She envisaged them both lying at the bottom of the stairs in a tangled mess, his hip re-broken and her body with brand new fractures.

After a few weeks, the constant terror was too much for her. The downstairs toilet her mother had installed when they both retired had turned out to be a godsend. At the time Jo hadn't really wanted to hear about how it was sometimes difficult to get in from the garden in time once you reached their age, but the forethought was something she would kiss her for now if she were still around. Its presence got her father through the days, but it didn't take away that fear of the wooden mountain each night.

The district nurse had agreed with her assessment. Her father hadn't. He had used a few choice words that she had never heard him say before, to express said disagreement. The whole meeting had been an uncomfortable one. Jo wasn't sure what the policy was for patients who verbally abused people these days, but the nurse shrugged it off with better grace than she would have managed. It was agreed. The dining room at the back of the house would be converted into a bedroom for her father. Because of his protests, they had stopped at getting him a hospital-style bed in there. Apparently, the threat of him killing himself because 'he might as well be dead if they were going to treat him as if he was dying' had been enough to convince them both.

The good news was, he had settled into the new routine soon enough. Which meant, thankfully, Jo could get the rest she needed. Tonight had been interesting, but she was ready to call it a day. Once the excitement of the procession had worn off, the reality of fighting her way through the crowds with the wheelchair to get back to the car had taken its toll. People were such rude arseholes. That was what this whole experience with her dad had taught her. 'Do you need anything?' she asked, as he settled down into his chair.

'No. I'm just going to try to crack the crossword and then I'll be off to bed myself. Twenty-one down is on the tip of my tongue.'

'I'm going to make a cup of tea to take up with me. Do you want one?'

'Yes, please, if you're making one. Maybe with a bit of brandy in it?'

'Are you allowed brandy in it with your medication?'

'Probably not. But if you do everything the doctors tell you to then you have no life at all. Just a tot. Not too much. But enough that I can taste it,' he called after her, as she walked through to the kitchen.

As the kettle boiled she leaned against the work surface and thought about the evening. Her mind relived the conversations, most of them unexpected. Emily was adorable and so was her aunt. Jo thought it might be the first time she had seen Kayleigh smile since they had met. From the moment Jo had made the announcement of who she was in the bookstore, that smile had disappeared.

Could Rob be right? Were the two of them really just friends? They had seemed so close, but try as she might, Jo couldn't come up with a reason why he would lie about something like that. He hadn't said outright that Kayleigh was a lesbian, but his insinuations weren't going to win him any subtlety of the year competitions. Jo looked down at herself. Perhaps it was the boots that had been giving off the gay vibes. She'd bought them at Maddy's suggestion after all...

The kettle turned off with a loud click, bringing her back into the real world. She made the two cups of tea – decaffeinated, even though her dad swore he could tell the difference until she had started lying to him about it — then added a dash of brandy to his. She was about to screw the cap back on the bottle when she added a generous splash to her own mug as an afterthought. One wouldn't hurt. The mulled wine had been quite nice after all. This was practically the same thing.

She carried them through to the living room, where her father still hadn't found the answer that was on the tip of his tongue. She placed the mug down on his tray and debated asking him what the clue was. No, it was better if she went to bed, rather than get embroiled in a long, drawn-out conversation.

'Thanks Love,' he said, nodding at the mug. 'I can smell the brandy from here, so you must have done it right.'

'There's a little bit in mine too,' she confessed.

'Good girl. You deserve a treat.' He looked up at her with a smile. 'You look happier than you have done for days.'

'I feel it. I think. Mainly I'm just tired.'

'Pushing this old man around can't be easy on the arms.'

'Or the legs. Bloody cobblestones.'

'Couldn't agree more. Friend to no one. Look pretty, but the moment you have a wheelchair or a stick they'll be the death of you.'

'Remind me never to break my leg around here then.'

'I'm glad though.'

'That I haven't broken my leg?'

'No. Don't be daft. That you look happy again. I was starting to get worried.'

'You don't have to worry about me.' Jo shrugged. It was a strange thought. For years she had been so completely independent of her family, needing them for neither encouragement or judgement.

'But I do. That's what parents do, no matter how grown-up their children get. But tonight? I've got to say, I'm proud of you.'

'You are?'

'Yes. I probably never told you enough. But tonight, I know you did something that most people wouldn't do. I don't know many people who wouldn't justify what they'd had to do or walk away. You've made a decision using your conscience and not your bank balance. You're a rare and special person for that.'

'Not as rare and special as her.'

'Soft spot for her after all then.'

'I never said that!'

'You didn't have to. I could see it written all over your face the moment you saw her. You lit up like a Christmas tree. Not hers, of course, from what you've told me.'

'That was a low blow.' Jo couldn't help but smile regardless. 'She's out of my league. But if I've got a chance to make her feel a bit happier, then I'll take it. And if not for her, then for Emily.'

'She's a special woman, I won't deny that. There aren't many people who would take on what she has and deal with it with such good grace too. But that doesn't mean she's out of your league.'

'You have to say that. You're my dad.'

'I've always been honest with you Jo. About everything. I wouldn't give you false hope for tomorrow just to make you feel better for today. She's pretty. Clever. And clearly with a good heart. She'd be good for you. I don't expect you to spend the rest of your life here looking after me each night.'

'Don't talk like that. I'm happy to be here.'

'And I'm happy to have you here. But that doesn't mean I expect it from you.'

'I'm not sure she'll forgive me this side of Christmas. Maybe not next year either.'

'Well only time will tell on that one. Molasses.'

'What?' Jo nearly dropped her tea, fear that he was having a stroke or late onset Tourette's taking hold.

'Twenty-one down. Molasses. Told you it was on the tip of my tongue.' He snatched the pencil from the table and proceeded to fill in the boxes. 'Now, off to bed with you. Big day tomorrow.'

'You're mad,' Jo said with a chuckle, leaning down and placing a kiss on the top of his head. His once brown hair was now brassy grey, but he still had more of it than most. 'See you in the morning. Don't forget to shout me if you need anything.'

'I'll be fine. Goodnight Love. See you in the morning before you go.' He gave her the briefest smile and then returned to the paper. She could see he still had two more clues to discover. That would be enough to see him through his cup of tea and off to bed.

She climbed the stairs, her legs like lead. She'd dressed warmly, but standing on the cold pavement took its toll regardless. Besides which, she was sure she had pulled a muscle in her back getting the wheelchair off the curb one time. She'd misjudged the drop and she'd fought to stop the wheelchair sliding out of her grip and over the toes of some poor unsuspecting stranger.

Her father's words echoed in her head as she entered

the bedroom that had been her childhood sanctuary. Through the teenage years, all those fears about what he would say if he knew she was attracted to women were concealed in this room. So many tears cried. First loves. Broken hearts. Trying to pretend she was straight when she wasn't. It had felt like the only choice she had at the time. University had changed everything for her. She had finally broken free of the expectations she felt her parents had forced upon her. If they had guessed back then it was true, they had never said anything. But she could also see now that the weight of expectation had been one she had placed on her own shoulders. They had never insisted on anything from her, other than she be truthful, kind and happy. But those things didn't make a good recipe for teenage angst, so she had created another scenario in her head instead.

The boxes were still stacked in one corner of the room. It seemed silly to unpack them now, this close to Christmas. It made much more sense to simply wait and tidy them away into their new homes alongside any gifts she might receive. The decision absolved her of any responsibility as she flopped herself down onto the bed and took a sip of the brandy-laced tea. It made her wince. It had none of the gentle winter softness of the mulled wine she'd tasted earlier. Instead, it was harsh on the back of her throat. She added a bottle of the decent stuff to her mental list of presents to buy for her father. If he was going to insist on having alcohol in the house for her to steal, it might as well taste half-decent.

CHAPTER ELEVEN

Kayleigh's eyes felt as though someone had tried to glue them shut in the night while she slept. As she let herself in through the front door of the bookstore and flicked on the lights, all she could think about was getting her hands on another cup of coffee.

She thanked gods she wasn't sure she believed in anymore that Emily had gone to sleep quickly after her breakdown. The excitement of seeing the big man himself, followed by the crushing fear that he might not find her again this year, had led to her crashing out before the tears had finished drying. Her heaving sobs had turned into deep breaths and Kayleigh had, after what felt like a lifetime, found the courage to ease her arm out from underneath the small sleeping form and sneak back downstairs.

The cold tea had mocked her. As if chamomile was the thing she needed in that moment. No, she had needed wine, and as she glugged down the first glass, the tears had begun to fall for her too.

Experience should have taught her not to drink on the night of the anniversary, not to excess at least. The whole bottle hadn't disappeared, but she'd had more than her customary two glasses. The dehydration, combined with the floods of tears had left her with a thick tongue and a banging head when the alarm had jolted her from sleep.

Even Emily had moved around quietly. She could sense the caution in her steps. Clearly Aunty Webby had looked under the weather. Today was not the day to open the shop later, but she was seriously considering taking an hour to herself in the storeroom and either drinking coffee until the caffeine flooded her veins or just closing her eyes and getting some extra sleep.

Her hands shook as she spooned instant coffee into

her mug, spilling half of it onto the work surface. 'Shit,' she swore, throwing the spoon into the mug. How could she possibly face the day when spilling coffee could reduce her to such a broken state? She needed more than the three hours of sleep she had managed to get. Three hours, caught in snatches. She had tossed and turned for hours, watching the numbers change on the clock next to her bed. Sleep felt like stolen moments from the night, filled with dreams she did not want to be dreaming. Her sister, trying to tell her something. Her sister, lying there dead in the morgue. Emily, in the hospital, lost in amongst the tubes and wires that would keep her alive over the next few days and ultimately save one of her limbs but not the other.

Every moment she hadn't wanted to relive had come to visit her that night. No wonder she felt like death itself.

Emily hadn't raised the prospect of the name change again that morning. Despite lying awake most of the night, thinking about the long term implications of a question asked with such innocence, she still didn't know what the right thing to do was. She supposed, if she thought about it, the question may have always come. The timing had been unfortunate, but for a child's simple grasp on what family meant, it was a logical natural step. It was her own fear that had kept her from thinking about such complex issues.

A bang on the front door made her jump. The jitters were getting the better of her this morning. She looked at her watch. She wasn't supposed to be open for another forty-five minutes. Whoever it was would just have to go away and come back later. She was too tired to deal with anything else today.

As she took a sip on the boiling coffee, the bang came again, more insistent this time. Irritation flared into annoyance and she slammed the cup down on the surface, prepared to go and give whoever it was a piece of her mind. She stormed through the shop, past the darkness of the Christmas tree. Just looking at it was enough to push her over the edge. This year was the worst year since the one that that had turned her life upside down. This pain was different but it was insistent. 'We're not open,' she yelled as she walked to the door. The banging continued regardless. She threw back the latch and yanked the door open. An icy blast hit her from the street. 'Who—'

'Thank god for that, I never thought you were going to open it.' The woman in front of her stepped through the doorway, letting herself in as Kayleigh stared at her brazen entry. 'It's brass monkey's out there.'

'I'm sorry, do I know you?' Kayleigh looked the woman up and down. She was cute, in a soft butch sort of way. Bundled up in a thick winter hoodie, she stood there in cargo pants and workboots carrying what looked like, to Kayleigh's untrained eye, a toolbox.

'Not at all. I don't think.' The woman leaned in closer and looked her up and down. 'No, definitely not. I'd remember you. I'm Maddy. Friend of Jo's.'

'Jo? What has she got to do with this?'

'Pretty much everything from what I've heard. You must be Kayleigh, right?' She extended her hand and shook Kayleigh's arm vigorously. In her fragile state, she worried it was going to be pulled right off. 'Any chance of a cuppa?'

'I'm sorry. I don't mean to be rude, but I have no idea what's going on.'

'Not a lot if I don't get a decent brew inside me. I'm here to sort the electrics. We're going to get this show back on the road.'

'I...' Words failed. Kayleigh felt the world go wobbly at the edge of her vision. For a moment, she thought that the complete lethargy from lack of sleep was setting in. She was going insane. Hallucinating. That seemed to be the most likely explanation for all this.

'You might want to shut that door too. You're letting all the heat out.'

'Yes.' Kayleigh shut the door without thinking, mesmerised by the saviour in front of her. No, really. It must be a dream. 'Jo asked you to come here?'

'She did. Luckily for her, I had a day off today. I'm supposed to be out doing my Christmas shopping.'

'I'm sorry.'

'Don't be. I did it all online back in September. I just needed a good excuse to have the day off and the boss is a softie when it comes to things like that. I was planning to go down the pub for the afternoon, but Jo pulled in a favour.'

'She made you come here?'

'That's a bit strong. Jo doesn't make me do anything. But we've known each other for long enough now that we owe each other a few. She reminded me of that time she had to come and bail me out.' The horror must have shown on Kayleigh's face, because she hastily continued. 'Don't get any wrong ideas. It has only happened once and it wasn't my fault. I was being a knight in shining armour. It just so happens that I was the only one who saw it that way and my damsel in distress didn't actually need rescuing. Is the kettle in the back? I can make it myself if you want?'

'Sorry. I'm just…surprised. I thought that…'

'I get it, most women are surprised when they find me standing there on their doorstep. And you seem nice enough and everything, but can you stop gawping and get me that cuppa? These electrics aren't going to sort themselves and Jo will be here at five to sign them off.'

Kayleigh watched as Jo headed towards the back of the shop and into the darkness. She'd managed to steer clear of a nervous breakdown after Debra died, but perhaps it had just been delayed? Maybe this was what it felt like. Not depression or feelings of suicide. Perhaps, for her, madness took the form of an imaginary friend who came to solve her problems in exchange for tea. The tea bit seemed quite important to her.

The thought of tea made her feet move at last and she followed the woman towards the back of the room. 'Milk and sugar?' she asked far too politely, as if the vicar had popped round unexpectedly on Sunday after church. She prayed that Maddy would say no to the sugar, as she didn't have any in the back room anyway.

'Just milk please. Make it a strong one.'

'Coming right up.' Kayleigh retreated to the makeshift kitchen at the back of the store and focused on her breathing while the kettle boiled. Somewhere, the faint glimmer of hope was starting to appear. If this wasn't a nervous breakdown, then there was a possibility that things would be okay after all.

'Madness,' came a voice behind her, making her jump. She turned around to see Maddy, hands on hips, looking around the room. Her lips continued to move as she mentally calculated something. It was awe-inspiring to witness. Kayleigh might not have dated anyone in years, but she could spot a one woman wrecking ball when she saw one. 'How long have you had this place?' Maddy asked when Kayleigh handed her a steaming mug of tea.

'A few years.'

'I'm surprised this didn't come up in the paperwork.'

'I inherited it. Any paperwork was simply around the transition of assets.'

'But you knew about this, right? You must have.' Maddy began to drink her tea. Apparently boiling water was not something she allowed to stop her.

'I knew that it was a bit dodgy. It was on my list to get sorted, but I just never got round to it.' The more she said it to people, the more it sounded like a lame excuse. It was the kind of phrase that people used for everything they just didn't care about, from mowing the lawns to joining the gym. If she backed the statement up with 'looking after Emily' it somehow felt wrong, even if it was the truth. She was martyring them both and she was determined never to do that.

'That's the problem with these old buildings. You never know what you're going to find when you start digging around. Bits get done here and there and then you have to put them right once the building regs come in. Then you have to change them when someone else decides that the regs need to be updated. Bane of my life.'

'So can it be done?'

'It can, but that's not what you're asking me is it?'

'Can you do it before Jo has to sign it off?'

'Not properly. But I can do something that would work. Unfortunately, I think your old man, or whoever did the job in the first place, got it done by one of his mates.'

'Are you serious?'

'Let me guess. He was the kind of bloke who wanted the lowest possible price and the minimum you could get away with. Wanted to feel like he was getting a bargain?'

'Now you mention it…' Kayleigh felt the warmth creeping over her skin.

'Thought so. People like him are easy to fool. You offer a discount on a job that's easier for you anyway, but for not much extra effort you could have done it properly. You do a bit less work, make it sound like a major thing, knock a bit off the price, people feel happy. Trust me, I saw all sorts of things when I was training.'

'This sounds terrible, but I have no actual idea what is going on.'

'Oh. Yes. Sorry about that. Sometimes I forget people don't know what I'm talking about.' Maddy drained her mug and put it back down. 'Come with me. I'll need another one of those before I start, but then I'll have to turn the electrics off. It's not going to feel like a good day for you, trade wise.'

'What?' Today was one of the busiest days. She couldn't close up shop for the entire day, not even to save her charity event. A whole day's business gone would put her in the hole. 'What are you going to do? I mean, I appreciate your help, coming here to do this for me, but you have to understand. This shop is my entire livelihood. I have a…a child I need to look after.'

'Jo mentioned something about that, yes. Okay, I get that this is a big thing. How about I talk you through what I need to do and you can decide whether or not it's worth it.'

'Thank you.' Kayleigh felt a rush of relief. Maddy was truly a godsend. She reminded herself not to feel too happy until she'd heard what she had to say.

'Good. Follow me.' Maddy grabbed her by the hand and tugged her out of the makeshift kitchen and back into the main store. She banged the wall where the alcove began. 'This used to be the outside wall of the main building. Which means everything on this side,' she waved her arm expansively in the direction of the store, 'runs off one fuse box. With me so far?'

'I think so.'

'Everything the other side, that runs off a different fuse box. If I had to guess, they used to be entirely separate buildings, but without much of a gap between them. A lot of houses around here were built that way. It's the curse of an old village. Houses went up where they went up and if they were built good enough to last, they stuck around and got modernised and joined. Some of those jobs were done well, some were done badly. This one, in case you hadn't guessed it already, wasn't done well.'

'But why?'

'No idea. But the good news for you is that I can make this into two separate jobs. The one that you have to do to sweeten up Jo, and the one you need to do so you don't burn the chuffing place down at some point.'

'Is it really that bad?' Kayleigh was horrified. She didn't want to bring Emily into a death trap. Or herself, now she thought about it. There was nothing quite as terrifying to a book store owner as the thought of fire.

'No, but you don't strike me as the kind of woman who'll actually get it done unless I scare you a little bit.'

'That's unfair.'

'And yet here we are, having this conversation because you didn't get round to doing it in the first place.'

'You make a good point,' Kayleigh felt thoroughly chastised.

'But there is absolutely no reason why this single room can't go onto the main fuse box. Unless I uncover something really scary once I get going. The point is, I'm going to have to turn it off while I get it done.'

'The power to the whole store?'

'Yes.'

'Could you just leave me the lights or something?'

'It doesn't quite work that way.'

'Really? Is there no other option?'

'The other option is that I do a rewire properly to the other half of the building, but that won't be completed by the time you need it to be. It's your choice really.'

'Shit. Let me think about this.'

'Okay. You can make me another drink while you do. But don't take too long. It's going to be tight if we start right away. The longer you leave it, the less chance I have of actually being able to pull this Houdini trick off.'

Kayleigh walked to the kitchen, feeling the spark of hope she'd allowed to foster wither and die. This was impossible. How could she run a shop all day without power? It was stupid to even consider it. There were so many things that relied on it. She'd never really considered before that she depended up electricity to make it all work. She wasn't quite ready for an impromptu trip back to the dark ages.

The lights. They were the main thing. The bay windows were lovely and did let in some light, but at this time of year, it was barely enough to light the room more than a few feet back. She couldn't run the bookstore without adequate lighting. She didn't know much about health and safety regulations, but it seemed that would just be swapping one hazard for another. Not to mention a terrible customer experience. If people couldn't see what they were looking for then they wouldn't buy anything anyway. She might as well shut the shop down for the day.

Candles? No. Only a desperate fool would fill a bookstore full of careless and busy people with candles. She dismissed the idea before it could really take hold.

Candles were madness, but batteries weren't. A memory came back to her. A single overnight camping trip she had taken with Emily before they'd both decided that it was not for them. It had seemed a good idea at the time and she had wanted Emily to experience all the same things the other children did, but the midnight trip to the toilet block had turned out to be more than either of them could take. They had packed up the following day and cut the trip short. Kayleigh had made her a makeshift tent in the living room and they had watched TV and ate ice cream from under it. The experience was a significantly less stressful one.

But the camping lamp she had bought for the occasion had been good and not particularly expensive. If Jo was coming at five, then she only had to keep the store lit for nine hours. That didn't sound too long.

The seeds of the idea began to take hold. If she could just make do for that short period of time, then she might be able to pull it off. It would be a logistical nightmare but perhaps if she could explain it to people in a way that made it fun...

A light bulb went off in her head. Wasn't it a traditional Christmas she always tried to sell them in the old bookstore anyway? One that wasn't too much around commercial best sellers. She had always wanted to preserve the history and heritage of her family business in a way she thought her grandparents would approve of. If she could be convincing, then this would just be an extension of that.

Damn, she was going to need some help pulling it off. But, if she did it right, she might just be able to. If it all went wrong, then she would lose a day's trading. Head or heart? She hadn't had to make a decision like that for such a long time. Head ruled and heart simply went along for the ride these days. But now, heart was demanding to have its say. Maddy had appeared to save her from this mess and she had Jo to thank for that.

She marched back to where Maddy was waiting and thrust a mug of tea into her hand. 'Okay, we're on.'

'Good girl,' said Maddy with a huge grin. 'I like you a lot. Shame, Jo would kill me.' With that cryptic one liner, she turned away and headed for the fuse box. Within seconds, the room was plunged into darkness.

*

'Camping lanterns?' The man looked at her as if she was asking for aliens. 'You want to buy camping lanterns?'

'Yes. Or something like it.'

'We don't really keep any out on the shop floor at this time of year. It's not exactly camping weather, you know?' He looked out of the window onto the car park, where rain was beating the tarmac hard enough to bounce back up.

'I really don't have time to explain. Do you have any or not?'

'We might have some. Back in the warehouse. Let me look on the computer.' He ambled towards the customer service desk and it was all Kayleigh could do to stop herself from giving him a little shove to keep him moving. The outdoor section of the store didn't get much business, not even in the lead up to Christmas, and it would appear the days of inertia had seeped their way into the man's bones.

He picked at the computer, using two fingers to type something in. Kayleigh had no idea what, but the computer threatened to be as slow as he was. Eventually he looked up again. He seemed surprised she was still there. 'How many?'

'Ten?' In truth, she had no idea how many she would need. But ten sounded reasonable. Maddy had warned her that the whole back of the store would be roped off anyway, so ten would cover the main stands and the sales counter. Her next stop would be the stationery store. She had no idea whether you could still buy receipt books, but she was going to have to have something to offer those who wanted one.

'We've got twelve of that particular model in stock.'

'Fantastic.' Kayleigh was truly elated. This was the closest out of town retail park she could think of. If he'd turned her away, then she wasn't sure she had a plan b. The man nodded at her, pleased to have fulfilled her request. The silence stretched out until she began to feel a bit uncomfortable. 'So…?'

'Yes?'

'Can I have ten of them please?'

'They're not on the shelves. They're in the warehouse.'

'I think we'd already worked out they weren't on the shelves,' the smile on Kayleigh's face grew tight. She struggled to keep it in place while she mentally reached out with both hands and strangled him. 'Could you get them from the warehouse please? So I can buy them?'

'I'm not allowed off the shop floor. I'll have to call someone to come and get them.'

'Of course you will.'

'So that's okay then? You want ten of these?'

'Yes. Ten of those. From the warehouse.'

'I'll just call someone. Be with you in a jiffy.' He picked up the phone next to the computer and made an announcement over the tannoy. She counted to ten in her head. Then backwards. Then up to ten again. No, she still wanted to kill him. He put down the phone and smiled. 'One of my colleagues will be here shortly.'

'Thank you.'

She watched as he ambled off again. She assumed that meant it was up to her to relay the message to said colleague, if and when he turned up.

'Hi, can I help you?' A voice from behind made her jump. She turned around to see a young woman wearing a Santa hat, looking at her expectantly.

'Are you the colleague who's allowed to go into the warehouse?'

'That would be me. I can't go onto the tills though. Someone else will have to do that for you.'

'What a surprise.'

'What can I get you?'

'I need ten camping lamps. From the warehouse.'

'You're brave aren't you?' She too shot a dubious look at the car park.

'It's not for…oh never mind. Yes I am brave. Also, really in a hurry.'

'Of course. Which model was it?'

'Which model?' How the hell was she supposed to know? Wasn't that their job? To know what stock they had in, where it was and how to lay their hands on it? If she ran her store this way, they'd still be selling copies of *Beano* from 1994.

'Yes. We sell a few different types of camping lantern. We like to cater to everyone's needs.' She parroted the company line. 'Let me look on the computer.' Santa's little helper darted behind the counter and Kayleigh looked up around the room, searching for hidden cameras. She had watched Saturday night television like this years ago. Come the weekend, would the nation be having a laugh at her expense? Sisyphus himself had more luck than this.

'I really am in quite a hurry,' she tried again, as the girl wiggled the mouse.

'Yes. Sorry about this. Oh yes, it's here in the last search. Large family camping lantern. We've got eleven in stock.'

'Eleven? I thought he said twelve?' That meant someone had just bought the one remaining one on the shelves. Who was mad enough to be buying a camping lantern at this time of year? She twisted around, looking over her shoulder for the culprit.

'Did you need twelve?' the girl looked uncertain about what to do with this new information.

'No. Ten.'

'That should be fine then. I'll just go and get them for you. They're in the warehouse.'

Kayleigh opened her mouth to reply and then realised nothing good would come of it. Further engagement would only lead to more confusion and, quite possibly, the total loss of her temper. And sanity.

As the girl disappeared towards the back of the store, Kayleigh watched until her red hat bobbed out of sight, trying to make sure she wasn't waylaid by anyone else. Keeping two requests in her head seemed an unlikely scenario, given the customer service she had already received this morning. When she disappeared out of sight, the rest was now in the hands of the universe. Kayleigh pulled out her phone to distract herself during the wait. The time screamed out to her from the front of the screen.

She was officially mad for trying to do this.

Once there was no turning back, she had decided to delay opening the shop until 10am. There would be some unhappy customers, she was sure of that, but it seemed like the only option in the circumstances. Now it looked like that was ambitious in itself. She tapped on her messages app, pleased to see that there was an alert waiting for her there. She opened it up and nearly cried with relief: *Anything 4u. B there at 11*. Despite his determination to use only text speak — mainly because he knew it irritated her — she was prepared to let Rob get away with it just this once. Her plea for help had been answered. That meant she wouldn't have to man the cash register alone if it got too busy. If it turned out she was able to handle things there on her own, then at least he would be able to explain to the customers what the hell was going on.

The minutes ticked by and she began to rock back and

forth nervously, her eyes darting around the store in case she saw the Santa hat doing something else. It wouldn't surprise her in the least if she had been completely forgotten. But then she appeared, carrying a large box. Kayleigh didn't know if she should be surprised that she had managed to work out that it would be easier than trying to carry ten individual boxes. Not that it mattered. She just had to hope they contained what she needed and not, by some random stroke of bad luck, bicycle pumps or other worthless objects.

'Sorry it took so long,' the girl said, dumping them on the counter. 'We're not allowed to carry boxes down the stairs and the lift is knackered. They're all in there though. There are eleven. I didn't know if you might want that one as well, seeing as you're taking all the others?'

'Why not?' At this point, it just seemed easier to say whatever the people in this damn shop wanted to hear if it meant she got out of there.

'Awesome. I'll take it over to the till for you.'

Kayleigh dutifully followed the girl, weaving through the customers that were now starting to fill the store. It seemed there was a last minute rush for outdoor gifts after all. It must be a very particular person who would want something from in here. Either that or the patrons were particularly unimaginative and had just decided it would be easier to pop in when they did their shopping at the supermarket over the road.

As she finally escaped through the doors, the rain pounded down even harder. The clear skies they had been blessed with over the past few days had disappeared. It meant that it was a few degrees warmer according to the weather app on her phone, but if it was, she couldn't feel it. She struggled to cross the car park but managed to dump the box into her car without getting her precious cargo wet. The same couldn't be said for her. She wiped the damp strands of hair from her eyes and planned her next move. The stationery store in town and then she would be back at the store. She was nearly done.

It was then she noticed the words on the side of the box.

Batteries not supplied.

CHAPTER TWELVE

'What do you mean she's not there?' Jo rolled her eyes as Maddy filled her in on the morning so far. At one point she had put her phone down on her desk while she found her purse and doubled checked she had enough change for lunch without needing to go to the cash machine. When Maddy was talking about work, sometimes it was better just to let the monologue run its course. The chances of her answering the actual questions before she was done were slim-to-none.

Now, in amongst the drilling and cursing the work of her forebears, Maddy had finally got round to answering her original question. 'If she's not there, then where is she?'

'Buying some camping gear.'

'I'm not sure I follow.' Jo knew that she had taken a huge gamble in sending Maddy over to the bookstore without letting Kayleigh know first. Unfortunately, other than the store number on the website, she had no real way of contacting her. Not without showing her hand as the Facebook stalker she really was.

'Look around you Jo. We're in the middle of bloody bleak midwinter here. I'm working in the darkness. It's a good job I know my stuff.'

'Which is fine. I get that. But why is she going camping?'

'Who said anything about camping?'

'I swear if you don't give me a straight answer I'm going to come over there and…' Threats were pointless around Maddy. She wouldn't stand a chance. 'You mentioned camping?'

'I said she'd gone to get camping supplies. Specifically lamps. I was telling you how dark it is in here. And you owe me.'

'I know I do. You made me very aware of that when I was begging you to do this in the first place.'

'I undersold myself. This is at least a two day job under normal circumstances. Do you know how heavy books are?'

'Very?'

'More than that. While your secret crush is out there getting the things she needs so she can actually open the store today, I'm moving books around and pulling up carpet.'

'Don't call her that.'

'What? Your secret crush? Why, because you know it's true?'

'No. Knowing my luck lately, she'll come back and overhear you.'

'Does it matter if she does? She seems nice. I could put in a good word for you.'

'I dread to think what your version of a good word would be.'

'I might oversell you. You never know.'

'Chance would be a fine thing.' Jo paused, trying to determine whether or not to ask the question she really wanted to know. They were far too old to seek approval from each other when it came to dating choices, but Maddy had been around the block a time or two. When it came to women, she knew how to form an opinion. Hell, it seemed to be the season for throwing caution to the wind. 'What do you think of her?'

'Kayleigh?'

'No the Queen. Of course I mean Kayleigh.'

'She seems nice. A bit slow.'

'I'm not sure what you mean by that.'

'When I came in, she just stared at me for ages while I was talking to her. She seemed a bit shell-shocked.'

'You do have that effect on people.'

'Years of practice. Maybe I'm giving her a hard time. If you'd told her to expect me then she might have looked a little less terrified. Plus, I think she'd been crying.'

'Crying?'

'Yeah, she had that whole red, puffy eye thing going on.'

'She seemed fine when I saw her last night. I hope it wasn't because of anything I did.'

'Why on earth would it be about you? How paranoid can you be? I know you said you liked her, but I didn't realise you'd got it this bad.'

'I haven't.' Even as she said it, she knew that it was the most unconvincing tone she could have used. If she didn't believe it herself, then Maddy would see through it in an instant.

'Pull yourself together woman. You barely know her. You only have it on someone else's authority that she's even into women. For all you know, this friend of hers could be more than that and hoping to take part in a sleazy threesome.'

'Ewww. He wasn't like that at all. How did you even think that was a possibility from what I'd told you?'

'Stop being so innocent. That was how Tricia Sweet ended up tied to the bed in a sex club one night.'

'Don't be ridiculous. Tricia Sweet always ends up in these scenarios because she actively seeks them out. You know that as much as I do. Then she always has this strange story to tell but we all know she loved it.'

'I can't believe you dated her.'

'I can't believe I trusted you when you told me I should. Besides, it was one date. That does not constitute dating. The moment I saw the leather I was out of there.'

'So you say. She tells a different story.'

'What? You know, never mind. I am not here to talk about the seedy adventures of Tricia Sweet.'

'Oh you saw she had a DVD out?'

'Stop it. Shouldn't you be working?'

'I'll have you know I am working. I am trying to work out where I can put my stepladders up when there is a huge sodding Christmas tree in the way. I would balance it against the wall, but it was a health and safety inspector who got me into this mess and I don't want her to get me in further. Just doing my adequate risk assessments.'

'Oh who cares?' Jo had a moment of panic before she remembered she was ringing on her mobile and her call wasn't being monitored for quality and training purposes.

'You'll be taking bribes next. That's how it goes. One slippery slope after the other and then you're accepting backhanders for overlooking shoddy work.'

'Does that sound like something I would do?'

'For the love of your life, yes.'

'I don't even know now if you're referring to Kayleigh or yourself.'

'Much as I will forever hold a special place in your heart, I was referring to the glamorous bookstore owner. This really is a nice shop though. I didn't know places like this existed anymore. I'm not even into books, but I could spend a few hours here looking at all the old stuff she's got.'

'Well, you've got work to do. Tell me honestly, do you think you'll be able to get it done by five?'

'I wish I knew the answer. It's going to be tight. I was only half joking about trying to work out where to put my stepladders. Normally before we do any kind of job like this we have the customer clear the entire room so we can move around. If I find out that just one wire is in a place I can't get to then I have no idea what I'll do. Don't get me wrong, the chances of it causing a real problem are small, but the work was shoddy. I don't think it was done on the books. Good spot with the sockets though. A dead giveaway that things weren't up to code. You could get away with it on private property, but this?'

'I really hope nothing goes wrong then.'

'Oh, she's back. Do you want to talk to her?'

'No!' Jo panicked, afraid Maddy would throw her under the bus without a second thought. She wasn't ready, not yet, for talking to Kayleigh. That she was letting Maddy go ahead gave her some hope that she might one day be forgiven. She still didn't expect that today would be the day.'

'Are you sure? She might want to thank you.'

'And she might not. I'd rather not take the chance. She might seem nice and sweet to you, but you haven't been on the receiving end of her temper. If I say the wrong thing then she might throw you off the job and we'll be back to square one. I'll talk to her tonight, when I come round to sign everything off.'

'Your call.'

'Now get on with it. Good luck.'

'Thanks, I'm going to need it.'

'And remember, call me if she says anything you think I need to know about. I don't want to mess tonight up.'

'You're doing a site inspection, not going on a date.' Maddy didn't actually say the words 'get a grip' but it was abundantly clear that was what she meant. 'Later.'

The line went dead before Jo even had chance to reply. She had to assume it boded well that Maddy had been allowed to start work. It meant that Kayleigh genuinely believed they would be able to pull this thing off.

She leaned back in her chair, a slow sense of satisfaction coming over her. For all his faults, her dad had been right. Sometimes, you just had to do the right thing and let the chips fall where they may. If, for some reason, someone found out that she had done it and wanted to sack her for helping out, then that would be their choice. She could only defend her actions on moral grounds.

They didn't have to know anything about her crush. That was incidental to the proceedings.

Maddy was right though. She did have it bad. She couldn't even pinpoint the moment when she had started to make this woman the centre of every thought. It felt like it might even have been the moment she had walked through the door to the shop that first time and found herself enchanted not only with the building itself, but the woman waiting there.

Her computer made a loud bing, startling her out of her philosophical contemplations. With everything that had been going on over the past week, she had been all too aware that she spent too much time daydreaming and surfing the internet, looking for any piece of information, no matter how small, that she could use to plead her case with Kayleigh. Given that she knew herself well enough to understand that her behaviour wasn't going to change, she had decided it was a supreme act of cunning to set an extra loud notification so she didn't miss any emails that came through. That way she could always look responsive, without actually having to be. In the general lethargy pre-Christmas where anything that wasn't directly related to the event itself just seemed like an obstacle, her motivation for a job that had already almost cost her a relationship with the only available woman in town had sunk to an all-time low. Keeping her inbox under control seemed like a big enough step.

She leaned forward and read the title: Early Performance Review. That sounded ominous. She had assumed that given the festive season, it wouldn't even cross her line manager's mind to think about it until the New Year. Jo swallowed nervously, a sense of dread hovering somewhere nearby. It was her own guilt, she knew, that made her afraid to open the email. Only she knew about her impartial response to a case. Even if someone found out in the end, then the word surely couldn't have spread already.

The click of the mouse was loud to her ears as the email opened.

Hi Jo,

It has come to my attention that you will be on holiday for your three month performance review. As you are aware, during your probationary period, you are required to meet the conditions of this review satisfactorily and also a subsequent one at six months. This allows us to assess your work to date and allows us to offer any additional support you may need.

As you will not be available for the week your review is meant to take place, may I suggest we move it forward to the week before? I understand that this makes your review earlier rather than later, but during the following two weeks I have meetings with some local government officials that will have to take precedence. Apologies for any inconvenience this may cause.

Please let me know if you are happy to do this and I will send an invite to your calendar.

Have a very happy festive break if I don't see you before.

Jo sank back in her chair, a wave of relief washing over her. She'd forgotten when she'd taken the job that she'd booked some time off for that week. It was meant to be her decide-whether-to-stay-in-town week. The reminder replaced one sense of guilt with another.

When she had agreed to move back to help her father, his prognosis had been uncertain. Given his age and his injury, it had been impossible to predict whether she would still need to be around after four months. When she had moved back here it had felt the right thing to do and she didn't begrudge him for it, but she was leaving behind a whole other life. One she had enjoyed and felt fulfilled by. She had friends and a nice apartment. A social life that wasn't dictated by the gentle seasonal rhythms of village life. There were bars and restaurants and clubs within easy reach. Sure, she was getting a bit on the old side for the clubs, but she didn't look it and when you were single, there was no harm in keeping your options open. It was the exact opposite to the cosy life she was now living.

There had been, although she hadn't voiced it out loud to anyone else, the doubt that after all this time apart, she would even be able to live with her father without the two of them being at each other's throats day and night. There were times, during her teenage years when she had been particularly hard to handle, that their verbal sparring had teetered on the edge of downright nasty. Jo knew she shouldn't judge the relationship she had with him a decade ago with the one she could have now, but it was hard not to. Her last memories of them living together had been before university, if you didn't include that first and only summer when she came back to stay for the holidays. Things hadn't been much better between them then. She could, for that summer, put her hand on her heart and say that it had been entirely her fault. Her new-found freedoms had made her childhood home feel like a cage. By then she knew, one hundred per cent, that she was a lesbian. She'd indulged in more than one kiss to make certain. Self-acceptance was one thing. Knowing but not being brave enough to tell her parents yet was quite another.

She shuddered at the memory. It was so much easier for the kids today. That was what they always said. Popular representation on TV. Books that actually included gay characters weren't hidden away in their own section at the back of only the largest book retailers. The world of sex online at your fingertips. So perhaps, in some ways, it was easier to work it out for yourself than it had been back then. For the older women she had met on the scene, they'd scoffed at how easy she'd had it in comparison to them. But telling your parents was never going to be easy. Fear of rejection, fear of fights, fear of outright refusal to accept what you were saying, were things she had faced and this generation faced and probably the next one would too.

At least now the two of them could talk about things openly. Her father still struggled to get the word 'lesbian' out of his mouth, but he acknowledged it in other ways. Like this thing with Kayleigh. It would have been easy for him not to mention the spark he saw. It would have been easy for him to just let it go and keep her with him, holding her close to him because he needed her right now.

So moving back with him hadn't been as bad as she'd feared when she'd first put that week aside, to either clean out her apartment ready to sell it, or to return and leave him to his own devices.

She had never once considered there might be another reason for her to stay.

A mental slap was what she needed to remind herself that nothing had actually happened between her and Kayleigh outside the constructs of her own imagination. And the interactions that had happened between them were certainly not enough to be factoring her into the decision-making process of whether or not she should stay. No, her focus should be on her own needs and those of her father. It was as simple as that.

Decision made, she sat back in her chair and tried to picture the look on Kayleigh's face when she signed off the paperwork and told her she could go ahead with the fundraising day and big evening event. The bright smile, perhaps even a hug of gratitude. It would be impulsive, friendly, but in that moment she would feel a spark of recognition and discover she would feel the same way about Jo as Jo did about her...

Yeah, she sighed to herself with a shake of the head, she was screwed.

CHAPTER THIRTEEN

The bookstore was buzzing. Kayleigh had been expecting a busy day simply because of the time of year, but it seemed that word of mouth was drawing people into the store. Her 'traditional Christmas shopping experience day' as she had so carefully labelled it to anyone who asked what was going on, had amused people no end. It almost seemed plausible too, if you ignored the sound of drilling and sawing and the fact that the back half of the store was out of bounds. Not only was it roped off, it looked like a bomb had gone off there. Books had been pulled off shelves to enable Maddy to move the free-standing book cases and get to the floors and walls they were blocking. There was even the occasional festive swearing going on, which Kayleigh couldn't bring herself to chastise Maddy for, even if some of the older customers were scandalised.

Maddy was doing her a giant favour and she could see it now. She had been confused at first when she returned to the store and had seen just how wide an area had been made unavailable to the public. She was soon enlightened by the sheer scope of the job that Maddy seemed to be single-handedly undertaking. They hadn't even discussed payment. The thought worried her, given the crazy prices she had heard from people over the previous week. But it was too late now. Maddy was working and it was getting done. Even if she had no regard for the careful shelf order. It would take weeks to get all the books back in the right place. Oh well, she supposed, it would give her something to do during the inevitable January lull.

Kayleigh hit dial on her mobile and tucked the phone under her ear. As it connected and rang out, she stabbed numbers into a calculator to work out how much she needed to charge the man who for some reason had brought an eclectic collection of four books of very different prices. If nothing else, her mental maths would be back to where it was during her school years. Only back then, she wasn't used to doing things in multiples of £6.99. 'Hi, it's Kayleigh Johnson, how are you?' She waited while the person on the other end of the line filled her in on a list of ailments she cared nothing about, bagging up the customer's books as she went. 'That's £18.96 please,' she mouthed at him. He looked dubious for a second — which made her doubt her own calculations, before reaching into his wallet and pulling out a twenty pound note. She took it from him and sorted out the change, feeling horribly exposed without the security of a cash register drawer to close. Like everything else, it was electric and there was no other choice but to abandon it. As soon as Rob arrived, she would have to take some of the money and put it in the safe upstairs. She liked to think the people in the village were good, honest folk, but at this time of year people without cash also got desperate. It would only take word to reach the wrong person and she would be in serious trouble. Her insurance policy wouldn't cover her for that kind of loss.

The woman on the end of the phone finally finished talking, so Kayleigh took the opportunity to speak before she thought of something else to say. 'I just wanted to let you know that the annual charity event at Johnson's Bookstore is back on again. Yes. Yes, same charity as last year. Yes, there have been a few problems this year. No, we're definitely going ahead. Fantastic. We look forward to seeing you then. Bye now. Yes, I would get that checked out. Oh, I've got a customer. Must go. Bye then.' She hung up and placed her phone down on the counter. This was going to be a long day.

The extended sound of an electric screwdriver caught her attention and she looked over to where Maddy was in the process of getting up one of the floorboards. She swallowed nervously. Was she tempting fate by ringing all the key people to get word out that the event would be back on again this year? Maddy had been moving things around for a few hours now and while there were plenty of signs of destruction, she wasn't sure she could see any real signs of progress. If she couldn't get this done, then there would be an event with one very forlorn looking Christmas tree, unlit and only able to be viewed from a significant distance. It was hardly the festive feeling that she had managed to create in previous years.

Once again, a sense of mild panic threatened to overtake the optimism she was trying so desperately hard to hold onto. Speaking to other people, telling them that yes, everything was going to go ahead after all, made it feel a little bit more real.

She began to move on to the next customer, once again with unusual choices at varying price ranges. 'Would you like a receipt? I'll have to write it out by hand I'm afraid.' Kayleigh had learned very early that morning that the standard response to the question *would you like a receipt?* was always yes. A Pavlovian response, she was sure, as most of them would only lose it in the bottom of their handbag. And really, who out of the many tourists that would be in here today would make the return trip to the village in the New Year to return something? Surely no one.

However, when she added the final part of the question, with the implication that it would take a lot of time and therefore hold them up from getting on with their busy day, the number of people who said yes fell drastically. After all, a book wasn't like the other gifts that people needed a receipt for. A book couldn't fail to power up, or have a part of it faulty. It couldn't be a size too small, or worse, an insulting three sizes too big. And if you didn't like it, you could return it to just about anywhere. These were the advantages Kayleigh had over other types of retailers and today, it was an ace she was more than willing to play.

'Yes please.' The man looked at her with a smile that

seemed to contain a touch of malevolence.

'Of course. No problem at all. It may take a few minutes. Is that okay?' She gave him a final get out. For a second he seemed to hesitate and she allowed her hopes to rise.

'I can wait,' he said after the pause, giving her that smile again. She tried not to grit her teeth. He was, after all, legally entitled to one. She began to write it out, starting with the title of the book, then the name of the author and the price. Despite the growing number of customers, she couldn't help but take her time. Using her best handwriting, she made sure every single word was clear. She wanted to make it clear to the man that if he was going to waste her time then she was more than willing to waste his as well, but he also seemed the type who would be willing to return the books just to check that the receipt was valid. No doubt he was hoping to get a disgruntled letter published in one of the Sunday newspapers if it wasn't, highlighting the scandal of this independent venture ripping off unsuspecting members of the public.

This fantasy played through her head and she totalled up the cost of the books and did it a second time to make absolutely sure. She wasn't surprised when he checked it himself before handing over his money. She made a show of counting out his change and then resisted the urge to raise her middle finger at his retreating back when he left the shop. As he opened the door, her thoughts were replaced by the arrival of her knight in shining armour. It wasn't so much as the man himself, but more the tray he was carrying.

'Wow,' said Rob, making his way around the counter and depositing a large paper cup of coffee in front of her. 'The place is really busy.'

'You are a lifesaver.' Kayleigh took a sip from the cup, pleased to discover that a trek down the street in the cool winter air had already reduced it to drinking temperature. She guzzled greedily, not caring about the strange whistling noise the lid was making at the rapid flow of liquid from the cup to her mouth. It had been a long morning and no electricity meant no kettle.

'I got a tea for our new friend over there.'

'I'm sure she'll appreciate it.'

'Milk, no sugar right?'

'That was what she demanded at some ungodly hour this morning, so I can only assume she is more than willing to have it now.'

'Do you want to take it over to her?'

'Why would I?' Coffee back down on the counter, Kayleigh was already stabbing at the calculator again. At least this customer was one from the village and would probably give her a free pass on the whole receipt thing.

'She looks a bit intimidating.'

'Really? I think she looks quite friendly.' Kayleigh didn't even glance over.

'Have you seen the size of that thing she's holding? What is it anyway?'

'I thought men were supposed to be fascinated by fast cars and power tools? I assumed you would know.'

'I work in a bank. Why on earth would I know about power tools? Anyway, it's lucky for you that no one wants to get a mortgage at this time of year. It's bad enough buying presents, no one has the energy left to think about buying houses.'

'When do you have to get back?'

'I can stay for a few hours to get you through the worst of the rush. I played the charity card with the bank manager. Her second cousin almost lost his leg to meningitis a few years back, so she was willing to go for it. She knows I'll only kick up a fuss if she puts me behind the counter while I've got nothing to do, so it's a few less hours she'll have to pay out in salary this month.'

'Oh Rob, I didn't mean for you to have to do that.'

'I don't mind. Seriously, I would rather deal with your customers than ours. Do you know what it's like when you get stuck with someone banking the takings from their store? It takes forever and they've never got it right. I hope you're better than that.'

'I do sometimes get it wrong,' Kayleigh admitted with a slight smile. 'It will be a miracle if the books balance after today. Anyway, go give Maddy her tea. She's been working flat out for hours now.'

'She has?'

'Oh yes. I know it looks like there's still a long way to go, but she really hasn't stopped. She's earned that drink.' Kayleigh turned back to the customer as Rob wandered over to where Maddy was balancing on a step ladder. Despite being more than happy to leave Maddy to her own devices all morning, she couldn't help sneaking a glance in her direction now. True to form, Rob didn't simply hand the drink over and then return. Within minutes, they had struck up a conversation and Kayleigh tried not to let paranoia get the better of her. Eventually, he ambled back when he remembered that he was here to help, not to distract everyone else.

'She seems nice.'

'What did you expect?'

'I don't know. I thought Jo seemed very nice when I met her last night, but everything you said about her painted a very different picture. So, if you were right and I was wrong, then there was every chance her friends would be as terrible as she was.'

'Shhh, she might hear you.'

'Over the noise she's making? I doubt it.'

'Besides, just because she's nice, doesn't automatically mean that I've changed my opinion on Jo.'

'No?' He looked at her, and she could see it was with genuine surprise.

'We wouldn't be in this mess at all if it wasn't for her.' She gave a meaningful look at the calculator before telling her current customer the price. She double checked it again. It was right, but this was far too hard to do with the distraction Rob provided. She looked up. The queue was now nearly ten people deep and that wasn't a good thing.

'I think you wouldn't be in this mess if someone else hadn't tried to take a shortcut,' he continued, oblivious to her distress. He took a casual sip of coffee and looked around.

'Instead of arguing with me about how we got here, what about helping me out?'

'Of course. Why didn't you say something?' He shrugged off his coat and placed it on the shelf behind the counter. He took a few extra seconds to make sure he had folded it correctly. Kayleigh tried not to hit him.

'I need you to start serving.'

'The customers?'

'Yes, the customers.'

'But the till isn't working.'

'Thanks for pointing that out, Einstein. Just calculate the total price of the books, offer a handwritten receipt and then take the money and give the change. My Saturday girl could do it, so surely someone who deals with millions of pounds in loans each day should be able to handle it?'

'My mental arithmetic is terrible.'

'Use a calculator you idiot.' She had to stop herself from laughing at the look of horror on his face. Clearly when he had offered to help, the actual prospect of what that might include hadn't crossed his mind.

After a few customers, he was soon getting the hang of things. Kayleigh's irritation and amusement both died down as they moved in rhythm together, getting through the queue as fast as they could. Rob was good at making them feel like they were part of a huge, fun experience, rather than a deeply inefficient one. Even the most impatient of people were put at ease by his jokes and relaxed personality.

The only problem was that they still couldn't move fast enough. With half the shop out of bounds, it only took a simple query to throw the whole routine out. Kayleigh knew her inventory well, more so than most shop owners would. She had loved books since she was a child. The store was more than a business, it was part of her life and she loved everything that was in there. Even books that weren't to her taste were part of a world she adored. So when people wanted to know if she had a specific thing in stock, it was quite easy to tell them yes or no. The problem came when the answer was yes and the book wasn't kept anywhere near the front of the store. If it was in the closed off area, it meant Kayleigh had to leave the counter and go to get it herself. It was the only way.

More than that, adding up the cost of the books and working out the change was the most time-consuming part. She understood the psychology of not using whole pounds to make customers feel like they were getting some kind of bargain, but it was working against her today. The calculations went both ways: the book costs themselves and the change given afterwards.

In a lightning bolt of inspiration, she grabbed a piece of paper and some pens from the drawer and scribbled out *3 for £15*. She would take a minor hit on the profit margin, but the time she would save in calculating the cost would be worth it to stop the queues forming and making her feel panicked.

'What are you doing?' asked Rob.

'Making your life a thousand times easier for the day,' she replied, writing the message out again on another piece of paper. Her eyes scanned the store, looking at the displays that were still standing and trying to work out where she could get away with using the technique. She was relieved to see that it was most of them.

'But how will I know?' he asked with a petulant pout.

'Ask each customer if they're part of the offer. If they've done it, then they'll know because they'll have spent ages agonising over which book they don't really want but makes it feel worth their while,' she whispered. 'Then ask me. I'll know which ones are included and which ones aren't. If anyone tries to fleece the system, I'll deal with them.'

'Sounds dodgy to me, but as long as you're going to handle the troublemakers, then who am I to argue?'

'Exactly. Besides, most of the time, it will just mean we'll be dealing with notes rather than pennies. And you know what? If it doesn't work, then I take the signs down and we carry on as normal. Shop keeper's prerogative.'

'Oooh, listen to you, Miss Business Owner. I wish I got to make all the decisions where I work.'

'Rob, there is a difference between making all the decisions and being a dictator. I know which one you'd end up being. Now get back to serving. Less talking to me, more talking to the customers.'

A few hours later, the signs were still firmly in place. The idea had worked, with only one customer trying to get away with something a bit naughty. Kayleigh had been firm but fair, keeping a smile on her face the whole time. Given the choice of paying full price for the books or leaving them behind, they had finally paid up. It had been uncomfortable, but the time saved with other people more than made up for it.

The lunchtime rush over, things settled down into a slight lull once 2:30 arrived. Despite the hard time she was giving Rob, she was grateful he had been there to help her through the worst of it. She had been optimistic at the beginning of the day that she would be able to get things done, but the reality had turned out to be quite different. Without him, she would have gone under. Now, they had things under control enough that she was even able to send him out on a lunch run for more drinks and some sandwiches. As she munched happily on ham and cheese, she tried to enjoy the way things had turned out. It had been a difficult day, but at the same time, she'd had more fun than she'd had in ages. Doing things differently had challenged her in new ways. It had been a long time since she had felt that from anything.

It was exhausting, but it was good.

'So, are you ready to admit that she might not be that bad after all?' Rob asked, bringing her back to the real world.

'Who?' Kayleigh tried to feign innocence but knew it wouldn't work. Rob had known her for too long to let her get away with that kind of thing. The best she could hope for was to buy herself a little extra time before she had to answer his question.

'Jo. You know who I mean. I don't think you could have found anyone who would work this hard for you. She's obviously pulled in a favour with Maddy.'

'Perhaps Maddy is her girlfriend? I know what you're trying to do here Rob, and it won't work. I'm not going to get myself tied up in knots because you think there's something more to this than there is. I'm not letting you put those kind of ideas into my head. I haven't changed my position. She got us into this mess. That's all I care about.'

'At some point, you're actually going to have to stop saying that and face up to the truth.'

'I know. But that doesn't mean I'm ready to.'

'I know what you're afraid of.'

'I'm not afraid of anything.' She was emphatic on that point and most days it felt that way. She had, after all, lived through some truly terrible times. She had been to hell and back and come out fighting. Emily had come out of it too and now the two of them lived each day as if they could handle anything the world decided to throw at them.

When he didn't reply, didn't call her out on the statement, she didn't prod him. She knew what he meant. Her world was a carefully constructed one, where she made the store and Emily her two priorities in life and she was more than happy with that. She worked hard and she was happy. She didn't need someone else to make her feel whole. She wasn't that kind of person. Sure, sometimes there were nights when she couldn't help but think about how long it had been since she had last been with someone, but that was to be expected. It was biological. It was human. It was nothing more than that.

But, in some ways, Rob was right. Another world, another time and place, things might have been different. When Jo had walked through the door, before Kayleigh had discovered who she really was, something had drawn her to the other woman. Even on the surface, before she spoke, there was something about her that Kayleigh had felt spark inside her. Then everything had gone wrong. Fast. But she couldn't deny to herself that the first little rush had been there. Was that the true feeling she should trust. Much as she hated that Rob might be right, she had been blinded to Jo as a person simply because of the thing she had done.

Last night, the woman she had seen pushing her father in his wheelchair had been a totally different person to the demon she had built up in her own head. Perhaps it was because they were outside the store, away from the constant reminder of how things had been nearly derailed this year. Without that to influence her, Jo had seemed warm and engaging again. Emily clearly didn't hate her either. Whilst it was never the done thing to rely on a six-year-old to be a good judge of character — especially given the horrors that they loved on the television these days — Emily was a good kid. She was naturally given to being upbeat, but Kayleigh had seen plenty of instances over the years where she had completely shut down on someone. They had seen a long line of consultants, therapists and overly sympathetic people in their journey together, and not all of them had received the instant thumbs up.

The more persistent tinkling of the bell above the door let her know that passing traffic was picking up again. She polished off the rest of her sandwich, glad of the excuse to take her mind off Jo and back onto the work. When she was serving customers, when she was ringing people to tell them that Christmas was back on, she was able to feel normal, more like her old self. She could forget there might be something under the surface she simply wasn't ready yet to face.

At 4:45, she dared to take a glance at Maddy. She looked dishevelled, her dark clothing covered in dust. Her hair flopped in her eyes and she looked exhausted as she pushed it out of the way. When Rob had been to buy them lunch, she'd only take the time away from the job to wolf the sandwich down. As soon as the last crust was popped into her mouth, the gloves went back on and she started again. As the hours had ticked by, Kayleigh had really begun to appreciate the level of effort she was having to put in. At times, she had been tempted to send Rob over to help, but it was never quiet enough for her to be able to manage without him. Plus, she had a sneaking suspicion that his lack of even basic handyman skills would have driven Maddy insane within minutes.

Things over that side of the store looked a little less chaotic than they had done a few hours before. Although books were still scattered all over the floor rather than lined up on shelves, the carpet was back in place. Two of the bookcases had been moved back to the wall they had come from and had been screwed back in place. The electricity had only gone back on briefly to test that everything was okay, some device emitting a deafening, high pitched scream which Kayleigh took to mean electricity was flowing to the sockets again. Just as quickly, it had been shut off, plunging them into semi darkness once again.

The first of the lanterns had given up just after four. It was at that moment Kayleigh had decided they would stay open only until five, rather than six. It would be yet another thing to hit on her profits, but she was prepared to lose them. Her fingers were sore and her body felt tired — physically exhausted — in a way it hadn't for years. Besides, she didn't want to be dealing with customers and failing light if Jo turned up and decided that she wasn't willing to give her a pass after all. With the sound of tools still being used, there was a good chance that Maddy's ongoing work meant they were not as close to being done as she desperately needed to believe they were.

She called out again to everyone in the shop, letting them know it would be shutting early so to make their way to the till with their purchases. The 3 for £15 idea had actually worked very much in her favour, with people taking advantage of it so much she had been forced to restock twice on some of the displays. Behind her on the floor sat Emily, who had been thoroughly enchanted with the lack of modern conveniences when she came in from school.

At two minutes to five, she was down to the last few customers. Her voice was hoarse with calling out to anyone new walking through the door, her voice full of apology but firm as she told them they were now closed. Some complained, some rolled their eyes in annoyance, others just turned on their heels and went back out the way they came. As the noise of the bell went again, she took a deep breath and began 'Sorry, we're—' She stopped when she realised who had walked through the door. Jo gave her a small smile and a wave. Another one of the lanterns, already giving off nothing more than a dim light, gave up.

Kayleigh tried to ignore her stomach doing an unexpected back flip. 'That's £15 then please,' she said to the customer in front of her, embarrassed when her voice turned into a little squeak. The woman looked at her, taken aback, but handed over her money. 'Would you like a receipt? I'll have to write it out by hand.' Kayleigh spoke slowly this time, in calm and deliberate tones, in an attempt to redeem herself. The woman shook her head no and Kayleigh almost kissed her with relief.

When she'd bagged up the final customer's purchase, she followed her to the door, happy to be able to lock it behind her. They were done for the day. If nothing else, no matter what happened next, she had made it through the hardest day of trading she had ever experienced in her life. She leaned back against the hard wood. She would need to dig deep to find the mental energy to deal with the next twenty minutes.

The lights went on.

They were no brighter than on any other day, but after hours spent in semi-darkness, she found herself squinting. She blinked, allowing her eyes to adjust before she looked over towards the back of the room. There, like a sign, the Christmas tree glowed brightly, the lights above it turned on, and the fairy lights giving their white and red twinkle from in amongst the branches. Through the darkest of times, there was her beacon of hope, alight once more.

'It's on,' laughed Emily from behind the counter. To see her little face light up with such innocent joy made everything she had suffered through worth it.

Kayleigh looked towards the back of the store. Jo and Maddy were caught up in discussion. Despite the casual clothes, Jo was here on business. The pieces of paper the two of them were looking at were official documents. She needed to remember that. There was nothing personal about this visit.

It was just business.

She was grateful Rob wasn't here. He would be able to read her mind as she looked across the store. She swallowed, the warmth in her belly growing as Jo shrugged out of her jacket, throwing it casually over a shoulder-height bookcase that would soon need to be restocked. She looked fantastic in her jeans and winter jumper, tight in all the right places. Kayleigh caught her thoughts a moment too late. She hadn't thought about anyone in that way for years.

She lifted her line of sight from the jeans upwards and saw that whatever the two of them were talking about, it looked more like a disagreement than a friendly conversation. Kayleigh's heart sank. Yes, there was definite finger jabbing going on and one piece of paper in particular seemed to be bearing the brunt of it. The prospect of having to call all those people again and tell them that actually, she had been completely wrong, the charity event wouldn't be going ahead again after all, filled her with embarrassment. It was more than just a personal shame; she wouldn't be able to expect people to take it seriously next year. What had started out as a health and safety violation could be the nail in the coffin of the charity event forever.

Emily was also looking in their direction with her head tilted in curiosity. Her fascination with the lights had quickly given way to uncertainty about the adults. Kayleigh watched as she came out from behind the counter to get a better view. Maddy was standing with her hands on her hips. There was a definite eye roll too. Whatever Jo was complaining about, the two of them couldn't agree on.

Kayleigh decided she couldn't put off getting involved any longer. After everything that had happened before, she didn't know if it would even help if she joined in the conversation. So far, she had been spectacularly bad at saying the right thing — or even a nice thing — when it came to Jo. If she'd spent the day putting herself through hell for nothing, then she knew that it would be a struggle to control her temper. As she walked towards the back of the shop, Emily grabbed her hand as she came past the till. Feeling the tiny warmth in hers gave her some reassurance, and the two of them carried on to face whatever may be.

'Is everything alright ladies? I see we have light and power.' She smiled what she hoped was her nicest, friendliest smile. Years of working with customers had given her some ideas about conflict management after all.

'Fine,' said Maddy.

'We're getting there,' said Jo, then shot a censorious look at her friend. 'Can you give us a few minutes please? There's a tiny wrinkle we just need to iron out.'

'Oh, okay. Sure.' Kayleigh backed away. The two of them knew each other well enough to deal with it themselves. She took hope from the word tiny. Wrinkles that were tiny were surmountable, surely?

After another five minutes, the two of them seemed to give up debating. Maddy threw her hands up to the ceiling and walked away. Jo disappeared behind the Christmas tree.

'Is everything okay?' Kayleigh asked, as Maddy walked over to the counter and leaned against it. She was more dirt and sawdust than clothes at this point and Kayleigh's heart went out to her. It had been a tough day on them both.

'Jo is just being Jo,' she replied, as if that explained everything. Kayleigh looked at her, hoping that her silence would prompt further information. 'Look, this whole thing was a favour. She didn't tell me about it until last night and for her, because she asked me to, I left home at five o'clock this morning and busted my metaphorical balls getting this shit done.'

'Which I am very grateful for.'

'Thanks. I know you are. But I forgot my book.'

'Your book?'

'Yeah, to sign off the work. With everything else going on, I left it in the van I use for work. I came here in my car. Just grabbed the stuff I needed.'

'Oh.' Kayleigh thought she could see the problem. 'Let me guess, she needs to see the certificate as part of her paperwork?'

'You guessed it. I've told her I'll mail it to you in the morning, but she's just being a pain. I've told her to check that everything else is done while I come over and cool off. Sometimes, we start to rub each other up the wrong way, then we just keep going for the hell of it. Sorry kid. Don't use that word.' Why she had the problem with 'hell' when she'd already sworn and talked about her metaphorical balls Kayleigh couldn't imagine and decided not to ask.

'So what happens next?'

'Same as always. We give her a few minutes to get her head out of her own ar— backside and come round to my way of thinking.'

'Does that really always happen?'

'Ninety per cent of the time. And it will this time. She's just a stickler for doing things properly. Which is what got her into this whole situation in the first place. She was just being good at her job.'

'I suppose you can't blame someone for being good at their job.' Even as the words came out of her mouth, she knew they were the exact opposite of what she had been saying for the better part of a week. Damn Rob. It was entirely his fault for getting into her head, she was sure of it.

'True. Forgiveness is a virtue.' Maddy gave her a smug smile and Kayleigh wondered how much she knew. The seed of the idea Rob had been planting took hold. Maddy had gone above and beyond because Jo had asked her to, but why had Jo cared so much?

A cynical little voice told her it was because she must have discovered that the whole thing was more than just so she could sell books. It was nothing more than guilt at having seen and met Emily. That was a perfectly valid reason to pull out all the stops. No one liked to have a guilty conscience and most people would do what it took to assuage one. Especially at Christmas.

Yes, that could be all it was. Nothing more. Nothing emotional.

After a few more minutes, Jo decided to finish what she was doing and join them. She gave Maddy the side eye and then turned to Kayleigh. In those few seconds before she spoke Kayleigh held her breath, hardly daring to believe that she might actually say yes. In the end, she couldn't wait any longer. The anticipation was killing her slowly. 'Well?'

'There were a few things on the list. Most of them are done. A missing certificate for the electrics is a serious thing, but as I happen to know where the particular electrician in question lives and am willing to hunt her down if she fails to send the certificate and I lose my job, I'm going to bend the rules and say I've seen it.'

'And everything else?' Kayleigh waited for the other shoe to drop. Jo's face was so serious and business-like, completely at odds with her casual clothes.

'Once those books have been put back on the shelves and the place is tidied up so it's not a trip hazard, everything will be fine. I'll put through the paperwork first thing tomorrow morning. Congratulations Ms Johnson, you're good to go.'

'Are you being serious?'

'Completely.'

'Thank you!' Kayleigh felt the tears forming and they fell before she could even attempt to hold them back. 'You have no idea what this means to me.'

'I think I do,' Jo said with a smile. 'I'm sorry you had to go through all this.'

'I suppose you were just doing your job. I wasn't particularly fair to you. Did you hear that Emily, we can do our big Christmas party again this year.'

'Cool. Will the newspaper man be there again?'

'I don't know. Maybe. But you have to make sure you tell all your friends at school tomorrow that we're going to do it after all. Then they can get their parents to bring them if they want.' It was devious, but it was the best marketing tool there was. Parents tended to be indulgent this time of year. 'Tell them Santa will be there to give out some presents.'

'Okay. I like it when the tree has its lights on. It was boring before.'

'You are right. Christmas trees are meant to have lights.' She swept Emily up in her arms and gave her a big hug. With the inspection complete, she felt the weight of the world had been lifted off her shoulders. 'You will come won't you?' Kayleigh looked at Jo. A not so subtle cough next to her reminded her that they were not the only ones in the room. 'Both of you. Obviously.'

'I'd love to,' said Jo. 'I'm sure Dad would as well.'

'He's more than welcome. Maddy?'

'Much as I would love to, I have plans for tomorrow night.'

'That's a shame. Well, if you change your mind, you know you are always welcome.'

'Thanks. But a date is a date and I don't like to let a lady down. And this particular lady isn't into cosy village scenes if you know what I mean.' Kayleigh wasn't sure that she did, but with Emily's tiny ears so close by, she thought it better not to seek clarification.

'How much do I owe you?' Kayleigh braced herself for a figure she wouldn't be able to afford without dipping into her savings. True, she should have thought to ask before Maddy even started, but the whole thing had been like getting caught up in a whirlwind. It was underway before her brain had even kicked into gear. She'd watched the woman work hard all day. She'd done her best and earned her money. Some of the cowboys she'd called had quoted her multiple thousands.

'I'll do you the parts at cost price,' said Maddy, looking at the back of the store as she mentally tallied up the work.

'That's very good of you.'

'It's actually very good of my company, but if you don't tell them then neither will I.' Maddy gave her a cheeky wink and she couldn't help but laugh in response. 'Can you do cash?'

'I really shouldn't be listening to this,' muttered Jo and walked off to pretend to look at some of the books on the history of the Cotswolds that were always close to hand.

'I think so.' It wasn't her usual way of doing things, but nothing seemed to be lately. And it was up to Maddy what she did with the money anyway.

'In that case, let's call it an even thousand.'

'What?'

'A thousand. Is that a problem?'

'No. I mean, I know it's a lot of money, but I was expecting you to say more than that.'

'I can raise the price if you want me to, sugar. That was a tough day's work.'

'No, a thousand is fine.' Normally, she wouldn't have that kind of cash to hand, but today had turned out to be a good day. She should do crazy things and get Rob to help her out more often. She would be able to pay Maddy out of the takings. It would all be okay.

Two days ago, she hadn't dared believe that okay was a possibility. Now, she could allow herself to breathe again. She looked over to Jo, unsurprised to see that Emily had joined her. The two of them were talking in hushed voices, heads close together. Yes, Emily had taken a shine to this woman who had walked into their store and their lives, turned everything upside down and then righted it again. It was almost too much to process.

As she waved them goodbye to them both a few minutes later, a strange sense of peace settled over her. It was a feeling she never usually got this time of year. Even on the happiest of days, peace was never what she felt. The reminders of what could have been — what should have been — were everywhere. But this was their life now and between her and Emily, they were going to make the best of it.

Besides, she had a charity event to arrange and in that moment, she was determined to make it bigger and better than ever.

CHAPTER FOURTEEN

It was with a curious combination of guilt and exhilaration that Jo snuck out of the fire door at the back of the building. Office hours would not be officially finished until 5:30, but tonight, getting to Johnson's Bookstore was her main priority. She'd promised her father she would take him too, so there was no way she would be able to make it there early if she finished on time.

She should, she knew, have cleared it with her line manager first. But with some staff already on annual leave leading up to the holidays and her line manager out doing a final site visit of the year, there was no one she could actually tell. At least, that was how she was able to justify it to herself. Besides, she'd taken a shorter lunch to compensate. Only about ten minutes shorter, but it was the thought that counted right?

If she stopped to think about it too much, Jo would barely recognise herself. Such a stickler for doing things properly, there was something about Kayleigh that made her want to cross lines and take short cuts. It was a freedom she hadn't felt since her late teens and with the sound of Christmas songs on the radio, it felt like the start of something special. Something new. She just hoped she wasn't wrong.

There was, after all, every chance it was purely in her own imagination. Rob had dropped hints, but she didn't know him. She shouldn't be relying on his word. Maddy had gone some way towards convincing her that he was a decent enough chap from what she'd seen. When they had left the bookstore together after the inspection, Jo had insisted on taking Maddy for a drink at the local pub. Maddy had agreed of course, never one to turn down the offer of a pint, but had worked out her cunning plan the moment she had started pumping her for information. About Kayleigh, about Rob, about anything she might have seen during her day there that could let her overwrought heart know if it was on the right track.

After the third question, Maddy had put her firmly in her place. In hindsight, Jo couldn't exactly blame her. The woman was exhausted, both physically and mentally, from doing a job that no sane person would do. So, despite what Jo thought, she had spent the vast majority of her day with her head down, unaware of her surroundings or what Kayleigh was doing. The best information she could give was that Rob had seemed very nice and had bought her two cups of tea and a sandwich and that when she'd stretched her back sometimes, she'd looked up to see the store was really busy for a tiny village in the middle of nowhere. She had then firmly endorsed the local ale and moved on to other matters.

Yes, Maddy had done her bit for building bridges — in an almost literal sense — so now it was up to Jo to handle the rest on her own.

Once she was far enough away from her office to stop worrying about drawing attention to herself, she turned the radio up high and blasted Christmas hits from the speakers. Her car was old now and she had to drive with the windows open sometimes, on days when it got this cold and damp, to clear the condensation from the windows while she waited for the ancient heater to warm up. She'd promised herself a new one for the last two winters whenever this happened, but she'd developed quite an attachment to it. This car had seen her through several girlfriends that were fun but went nowhere. Maybe it would see her through the next one. That would go somewhere, she mentally added, not wishing to add Kayleigh to her list of failed relationships.

A slouching teenager, dressed ninety-five percent in black and therefore camouflaged against the night, stepped out into the road in front of her, eyes down at the phone in his hand. She swerved slightly and swore at him. She watched as he jumped and remembered that the window was down and he had just heard every expletive thrown his way. Good. She hoped the surprise would remind him that he wasn't invincible and although he probably thought his parents hated him and he hated them — she thought she could reasonably make that assumption based on age, clothing and her own emotions from that time — that they would be devastated if he got run over at Christmas because he was more interested in whatever social media channel he was looking at.

She glanced in her rear view mirror. He was already staring at his phone again. Oh well.

When she pulled onto her father's driveway, she was relieved to have made it home without any further incidents and in good time. It would be nice to be home at this time every night, she mused, before realising she probably shouldn't get into the habit of bunking off early. 'Hi, I'm home,' she called as she walked through the doorway. The heat of the house blasted against her face, feeling far too warm after the chill of her car.

She took off her coat and boots. 'Hello?' she called again, when she realised there had been no response. Her heart began to quicken as she walked down the hallway and into the living room where her father spent most of his days. When she walked in she found him seated in his chair, body lurched forwards. 'Dad?'

'I'm trying to tie this blasted shoelace,' he muttered, frustration oozing out of every pore. 'I thought I could be ready when you got back so you didn't have to worry about me.'

'Dad, I can do your shoelaces for you. It's really not a problem.'

'I know. Help me back up.' He said nothing as she gently lifted his upper body into a seated position and pushed him against the back of the chair. 'At least I'm not quite incontinent yet,' he grumbled, 'although I suppose that's the next thing to look forward to.'

'Dad, you've done a great job in the circumstances. So what if you couldn't tie your shoes at the end of it? That doesn't matter.'

'I just thought you might like the time to get yourself ready instead of me for once.'

'Thank you. I really appreciate the thought.' She dropped a kiss on the top of his head. He could be the sweetest sometimes. 'I'm going to make a cuppa first. It's cold out there tonight. Want one?'

'Yes please. I've no idea how long I've been looking at my own knees.'

'That doesn't sound like a particularly interesting sight, I agree.'

'You have no idea. But I did spot where that biscuit I dropped last night went. It's sticking out from under the chair leg. Must've bounced.' He gave her a grin and she crouched down next to his chair. Sure enough, half a biscuit was poking out from underneath. She made sure to take it with her. At his age, the three second rule didn't seem to matter if you could brush the fluff off it.

Still, she brought him a replacement or two with his cup of tea and grabbed a handful to take with her when she got changed. She wanted to look good for Kayleigh tonight and a few biscuits at this late stage weren't going to do any damage. As she chomped down on them, she surveyed her wardrobe. Friendly, but casual. Smart, but casual. Cool? There were so many options and she wasn't sure which one was appropriate for an evening like this. The only thing she knew for sure was that she wanted to remove any hints of 'work Jo' from herself. She wanted to be there tonight as a new friend, nothing more. Kayleigh had started to soften towards her a little. No reminders of the person who got them into this tricky situation in the first place would be a good idea.

Once she was confident in her look, she checked her watch. Damn. She had taken longer than she wanted to create a look that could best be described as 'completely neutral'. She was sure other women couldn't possibly take this long to get ready when the most they were aiming for was average and normal. She took one last look in the mirror. A small pep talk and then they could go.

Unfortunately, parking turned out to be less easy that she had expected. There were several disabled parking spaces in the street, but they were on a first come first served basis. In a village where the local residents were predominantly in the older age groups, there were plenty of blue badge holders to go round. By the time she was wheeling her father up the high street, she was already feeling stressed and, rather grimly, a little bit sweaty from the exertion. Jo hoped this wasn't a sign of things to come.

Very few other stores were still open. Late night shopping simply wasn't cost effective outside of malls or city high streets. Here, people wanted to go home to their families more than they wanted to make an extra few quid for many hours extra work. Some of the store fronts were already in darkness, others had their windows only bathed in a faint light, reminders to any passersby on their way home from the pub of what their wares were.

But it wasn't the pub that was the hive of activity tonight. As she passed the newsagents, she saw people spilling out onto the street. She had no idea what to expect from the evening. In all their conversations and all the internet stalking she had managed to fit in around doing actual work, there hadn't been much information to be found about what the evening entailed. All the newspaper reports were about the amount of money they raised.

A makeshift table stood outside the building next door, a tea room closed for the evening. Inside, towards the back, she realised there was a light on and Kayleigh must have some kind of arrangement with them to use their facilities. The food and drink options couldn't be a wide range given the size of the table, but she concluded they must be of a good quality given the size of the queue lining up. The weather had gone in Kayleigh's favour; clear but cold. The very weather that made a hot drink and warm mince pie an almost irresistible proposition. It was still early.

Not for her. She had places she needed to be.

Jo manoeuvred the wheelchair past the queue, a young man who stepped out of the way for her helping to push back his friends so she could get by. It seemed the Christmas spirit was beginning to win people over. Schools had finished for the holidays and so had some parents. Some were working with a slower pace, others were rushing to get things finished before the break began. It created a unique sense of everyone coming together for this moment that only happened once a year. Jo couldn't call herself religious, but she could appreciate a season of giving and forgiveness. It was what she was hoping to find for herself.

She hesitated for a fraction of a second before pushing open the door and crossing the threshold that separated Johnson's Bookstore from the rest of the world. The warmth hit her first, bringing with it the noise of laughter and children playing. Once this would have been enough to make her roll her eyes and head straight back to the mulled wine, but now she found herself looking for Emily. Jo pushed her father inside and then they were in the midst of it all. The display tables had been cleared of books, instead trimmed with a festive winter green cloth and covered in decorations. A few teenagers with buckets were walking around taking collections. Kayleigh had mentioned hiring casual staff by employing those local high school students with a love of reading. It seemed she had picked the right ones if they were willing to give up their evening to work for free and help out here.

Jo had to remind herself to play it cool, instead of bobbing up and down trying to see over people's heads. Tonight wasn't all about her. It was about Kayleigh and Emily. And the children, she added as a mental afterthought. That was it, the children.

At the back of the store, the tree was lit up as it should be, in its full glory. In many ways, it still looked like a potential health and safety hazard or, at the very least, a crime against good taste, but Jo didn't care tonight. She simply wanted to be a part of it all. A part of village life and a part of Kayleigh's.

Next to the tree stood Santa, waving to the children and giving out occasional presents. If there was any kind of system, she couldn't work out what it was, but the absence of meltdowns was a good indication that it worked.

'Hi.' A voice behind her made Jo jump. She turned around to see Kayleigh standing there, holding two plastic tumblers of mulled wine. 'I jumped the queue for you. One of the perks of the job.'

'Thank you.'

'No problem.' Kayleigh smiled and Jo felt her knees go weak in a way that wouldn't be a good combination with the wine. She might have to turf her father out of the wheelchair so she could sit down if Kayleigh hit her with that thousand watt grin again. Jo stared for a few more seconds, before Kayleigh gave a subtle nod in the direction of the drinks.

'Oh. Yes. Thanks.' Mentally kicking herself, Jo took one of the tumblers and handed it to her father who, in the lost seconds when Jo had been gazing like an idiot, had been discovered by Emily and the two of them were now engrossed in conversation. She turned back and took the one intended for her, trying not to spill it when their fingers touched. Yup, she had it bad.

'I can't stay,' Kayleigh said, pulling her hands away and shoving them deep into the pockets of her jeans. 'I have to manage this chaos.'

'Of course. It looks great.'

'Thanks. Talk later perhaps? If I have time?'

'Sure. Go ahead. Oh, and thanks for this,' Jo raised the

cup. At the last second, she realised her hands were shaking and prayed that Kayleigh would assume it was due to the cold weather they had just been through to get here.

As Kayleigh headed back into the crowd, Jo watched her go. This was going to be a tough night. But, it seemed, she had been forgiven. Maybe not all the way, but a crack had appeared in that hard outer shell and Jo was prepared to take full advantage of it. The two of them had a connection, she had known that right from the start, but all the drama had got in the way. When tonight was done, she would have to convince Kayleigh to allow them to start again with all of the difficulties behind them.

A tug on her coat snapped her back to the real world. She looked down to find Emily grinning back up at her. 'Hi Emily. Are you having fun?'

'Lots. Aunty Webby is happy again too.'

'That's good isn't it?'

'She's been sad a lot lately.'

'She's probably just been very busy. Look at all the people here. That's a lot to do. Plus she managed to get Santa to come. That's pretty impressive.'

'Oh.' Emily looked over her shoulder and then beckoned for Jo to come down to her level. She bent forwards so she could whisper in her ear. 'That's not really Santa. That's Uncle Rob. But you can't tell anyone.'

'My lips are sealed.'

'He helps Aunty Webby do this every year. He says he's not fat enough to be Santa, but she says he is. But the real Santa is too busy, so he has to help. But you can't tell the other kids. They'll be sad.'

'Well it's very good of Rob to help out. But don't worry, I won't tell anyone.'

'He's still given me a present though.' Emily proudly held up a small box wrapped in bright red paper.

'That's the main thing.'

'Are you going to stay?'

'Yes, we'll be here for a while.'

'I'll see you later then. My friend Mozzi is waiting for me. She says that her parents are still going to make her go to bed at normal time even though we don't have school tomorrow, but I can stay up late. Bye Jo. Bye Mr. Herbert.'

With that she was gone, leaving Jo and her father standing there. 'Mr. Herbert?' she asked with a raised eyebrow.

'I think it's wonderful that some children these days still have manners. Must be the way she was raised. Kayleigh's done a good job, don't you think.'

'Hmmm,' Jo mumbled into her wine.

'Nice woman. Kind. Strong. Cares about the community. Shame she's alone, wouldn't you say.'

'Oh shut up,' Jo swatted him on the shoulder.

'Just pointing out the obvious.'

'There is no obvious.'

'My girl, from the way you were staring at her with your mouth flapping up and down like a fish, there was plenty of obvious.'

'Oh god, was I really that bad?'

'I've never seen you look at someone like that before.'

'It's not that simple.'

'I keep telling you. Make it that simple. Goodness, there's Terry.'

'Who?'

'Terry Gibbons. Used to own the farm on the way out of the village. Used to bring us fresh milk when you were a nipper. Don't you remember?'

'I don't think so.'

'Take me over to him. I want to have a chat with him about the Rotary Club for next year.'

'Sounds thrilling.'

'I never said you had to stick around. Go talk to someone your own age.'

'She's busy,' Jo grumbled, pushing their way through the crowd towards where the man who she had no recollection of was standing.

'Well offer to help. Or make new friends. You don't have to hover behind me all night like your only purpose in life is to push this damn thing around.'

'Are you sure?'

'Of course I am.'

'I've got my mobile on me. Do you have yours?'

'Yes.'

'Is it charged?' she asked suspiciously. This was something of a recurring theme.

'I think so.' He patted his pocket, as if that was all it took. 'I'll give you a call if I need you. I promise. Now go. I'm not completely useless.'

'Okay, okay. As long as you promise?' But he was already reaching up to grab Terry's hand and she knew she had been dismissed from the conversation.

Jo stood awkwardly for a minute while the two of them began to talk, before realising she should move if she wanted to stop looking like a spare part. In the close confines of the shop, it was starting to get warm and she tugged the top of her coat open to let in some fresh air. Yes, it was just the sheer number of people in the store, she told herself. Nothing to do with the mulled wine and the prospect of actively seeking Kayleigh out for the first time since her animosity had begun to thaw.

She moved through the crowd, apologising left and right for bumps and treading on toes. The whole village must be there. More importantly, she realised, the whole village was dipping into their wallets, the Christmas cheer getting them to part with their hard-earned cash. After coming so close to not going ahead at all, she could only hope she had played some small part in making it a fantastic success.

Towards the back, just before the Christmas tree displayed in all its glory, Rob looked like he was beginning to flag in the face of the long line of children. His beard hadn't quite slipped, but she could see traces of sweat glistening on his brow. Now she had seen the man underneath, she could appreciate the amount of padding he must be wearing under the costume. It would be like a sauna in there. Next to him, chatting animatedly to someone, was Kayleigh.

Jo took a moment to look at her. Really look at her. This was her big night and her passion for it shone through. She looked almost happy and that wasn't something she had ever really seen in all the times they had met before. That thought alone tugged on her heartstrings and redoubled the guilt she felt for causing all the trouble in the first place.

As if sensing she was being watched, Kayleigh turned and made eye contact. Jo's world froze for a second again and she wondered when Kayleigh would stop having that effect on her. A simple smile should not have the ability to disconnect the brain and body in such a way. She forced herself to give a small wave and saw Kayleigh begin to wrap up the conversation.

'It's really busy in here,' said Jo, when the two of them finally stood next to each other.

'I know,' Kayleigh replied, her voice almost too quiet to be heard above the din. 'My throat is getting sore from talking to all these people.'

'There's a few hours left to go yet.'

'I know. I'm going to be exhausted tomorrow. But it's worth it.'

'Pardon?' Jo asked, leaning in closer.

'I said it's worth it,' Kayleigh raised her voice again.

'Do you think you'll raise as much money as last year?'

'Fingers crossed.'

'What?'

'I said,' Kayleigh began before giving up. She gestured for Jo to follow her and began to move towards the back of the store. The crowd became a little less tight once they were clear of Santa, but it was still busy enough. They reached the roped off area and Kayleigh stepped through it.

Jo followed, knowing the space behind the Christmas tree all too well. The books towered above them on either side, a curious collection of old, cracked spines, long since forgotten. Hidden from view by the colossal number of hand crafted decorations and gifts, it felt like a private sanctuary from the hustle and bustle of the main store.

'That's so much better.' Kayleigh leaned against a bookcase, arms crossed comfortably across her chest. 'God, it's madness out there.'

'I'm really glad that it is.'

'Me too. We'll know tomorrow when I do the final count of the money, but so far it's looking like it could be the best year for us ever.'

'That's great news. Really. I mean it.' Jo gave her most sincere smile. Up until the day before, Kayleigh had been unwilling to believe that she felt terrible about what she had done. Jo had been given the distinct impression that Kayleigh thought she actually enjoyed causing the devastation, when nothing could have been further from the truth. She was about to discover if her grand gesture, in the end, had finally won Kayleigh round.

'I know you do. That was what I was trying to say back there. I haven't thanked you for making this possible. Maddy was a lifesaver.'

'I won't tell her that, it'll just go to her head and that's big enough already. It was the least I could do, after all the trouble I caused.'

'I suppose I should apologise to you for that too,' said Kayleigh, a half-smile of reluctance on her face.

'I'm sorry, I'm not sure I heard you.' Jo feigned deafness and stepped closer. She cupped her hand to her ear. 'Could you say that again?'

'Okay, okay. I said I'm sorry.'

When Kayleigh leaned in to whisper it into her cupped ear, Jo could smell her perfume, soft and sweet. The two of them were almost the same height and Kayleigh's eyes met with her own as she half pulled away. Jo swallowed nervously. The noise of the rest of the room faded away as she stood, paralysed by what could happen next, tucked away in their own little piece of Christmas.

Jo didn't know what to do. She only had Rob's word for Kayleigh's interest in her, if he had even called it that. He'd just suggested that the two of them should give each other a chance, that was all. She swallowed again, praying for some sort of sign that would tell her what to do.

She glanced heavenward, as if expecting God to be interested enough to send a word of wisdom her way, and saw above them a sprig of green and white. It was wrapped in fairy lights and from this distance, in amongst the twinkling, she couldn't tell if it was real or plastic, but it didn't matter. Kayleigh's eyes followed her own and the two of them stood under the mistletoe waiting for the other to make the first move.

This was her chance, Jo knew. She still believed, perhaps even more so after this evening, that Kayleigh was out of her league. But she also knew that she would never get a chance like this again and if she didn't take it, she would be kicking herself forever.

She took a deep breath, prayed that this wouldn't end in a slap like it had the last time she'd pulled this stunt on someone, and leaned in. At the last second she closed her eyes, not wanting to see a look of horror on Kayleigh's face if she had misjudged the situation after all. A slap was better than that, she reasoned.

Kayleigh's lips against her own were soft. The kiss was gentle, almost chaste, but it was more than a 'just a friend' kiss. Jo waited for Kayleigh to pull away, but instead she found a hand on her hip, pulling them together. The kiss deepened and Jo felt her world start to spin as she realised she was finally kissing the woman she'd been unable to get out of her mind from the moment she had set eyes on her.

Then, she was gone. The spell was broken.

'I'm sorry,' Kayleigh's hand flew up to her lips, as if surprised by what they had done without her permission.

'Don't be—'

'No. I shouldn't have done that. We can't…I'm sorry, this was a mistake.'

'Kayleigh, we should—' but before she could finish the sentence, Kayleigh had already turned away, moving around the Christmas tree that had served as a shield from the crowd and heading straight back into it.

It wasn't the first time Jo had kissed a woman who'd then run away in a moment of panic, but this one sure as hell hurt the most.

CHAPTER FIFTEEN

The evening had been a monumental success.

That was what everyone kept telling her, even as she fake smiled and allowed the panic to course through her. Only Rob noticed enough to ask her what was wrong. To which she had replied, quite honestly, that everything suddenly felt overwhelming.

Kayleigh stared at the ceiling, the light from the landing making shapes in the room visible. Outlines of furniture, picture frames on the walls, their glass reflecting the light out at strange angles into the room.

She reached out and turned on the lamp. Sleep was going to remain elusive for some time, so she might as well embrace the fact.

The evening *had* been a success, she reminded herself. That was what she should be focused on. She reached up and touched her lips. It had been so long since anyone had kissed her, she had almost forgotten what it felt like. A kiss that wasn't from a friend, or a sloppy display of affection from Emily. A kiss that had sparked instead a long buried feeling, kept somewhere deep inside.

Her first and only real relationship had not been a great success. At the time, she had walked away from it thinking she was heartbroken beyond repair and she would never be the same again. It had mattered far more than anything else. She rarely thought back to it these days, but in hindsight it was nothing in comparison to the loss of her sister and brother-in-law. If she'd wanted to know what real pain felt like, then that was it. By then, the heartache had already begun to lessen. Rob had told her all along it would, but in the acute agony of the moment it had been impossible to believe him. It had also been impossible to believe that she would ever want to find anyone else. Or that there would be anyone out there — any woman out there to be specific — who would feel the same way about her. She'd already made the decision that the village would always be her home, and slim pickings was an understatement. He'd told her that her time would come, but she hadn't believed him then, despite being right about her finding the strength to go on and heal.

She was also marginally annoyed that Rob had been right about Jo. The two of them did fit together well, if the spark of the kiss they had shared was anything to go by. If she hadn't so very recently got the electricity problem fixed in that part of the store, she would have wondered if it had finally broken and was sending tingles up through the floorboards and into her entire body.

With the duvet tucked up under her chin for warmth, she knew she only had herself to blame for letting it get that far. She'd seen the mistletoe above them, of course she had. A rebellious part of her had been debating whether she should take the risk when Jo had done it for her and absolved her of all such responsibility. But she could have pulled away then. She could have pulled away instead of leaning into the kiss, feeling it melt her body like nothing she remembered from before. She was the one who had deepened it and moved closer.

Oh, and she was also the one who had then run away, she reminded herself. Mustn't forget that part of it. Literally run away. Nothing about the experience painted her in a good light and she knew it. The remainder of the evening had been fraught with tension as her face remained frozen in a smile for others, while her eyes scanned the room for Jo at all times so she could avoid her and the hurt look she would no doubt have on her face. Those eyes would be the death of her, all sad and forlorn, like a puppy she'd kicked. She remembered it now from the first time when she had come in to apologise and Kayleigh had cut her down before she could even properly get the words out.

In hindsight, what the hell did Jo even see in her

anyway? She'd been nothing but a bitch to her right from the start.

She started it, a childish voice whispered in her head before she shut it down.

This kiss had been nice. More than nice. It was amazing. Jo had slowly won her round, with the way she looked after her own dad and the way she had been with Emily. So why on earth had she run away so fast Jo couldn't even give her a reason to stay?

She knew why of course, even though it was unfair to blame the little bundle of Christmas energy lying asleep across the hallway from her. Emily had been her sole purpose for living for so long, that a single kiss would never be enough to change that. It was true that the two of them had settled into an easy routine now, that they loved and cared for each other deeply. But the road ahead was paved with a lifetime of challenges and that meant she would continue to put Emily first for the next few years.

She wasn't stupid. She might not have many close friends, but she had watched her acquaintances in the village move through their grown-up lives. Loving, marrying, divorcing. Moving on to a new relationship was always a challenge when there were already children involved. Emily wasn't even her own child, although it hurt her to think of it like that. She loved her as if she was, but how could she expect Jo to take on that responsibility? She had no idea what it would be like. She'd only seen Emily on her good days, when her bright and sunny disposition was enough to light up a room. She hadn't been there through the pain, the tears. The harrowing sense of loss that sometimes still came to her after a bad dream. Yes, the road ahead was rocky and she wasn't naive enough to think someone like Jo would want to take that on. Who in their right mind would?

Was that nothing more than an excuse? It almost sounded like one. She couldn't deny she was afraid, but that had nothing to do with the fact she was just trying to be a grown-up. Right?

With a groan, she threw back the covers and got out of bed. She crossed the hallway, walking on tiptoes in just her socks to eliminate as much noise as possible. It had been another late night for Emily and they were all going to catch up with her sooner or later. There was no point adding to the exhaustion by waking her up in the middle of the night.

Despite her reservations, she couldn't help but look in on her as she walked by. In the light, she could see she was sprawled out in the centre of the bed, looking like a sleeping angel. Kayleigh never knew it was possible to feel this much love for another human being, but somehow, she did. Both legs tucked away under the duvet, it was possible to imagine that Emily had lived an innocent and idyllic childhood up until this point, rather than the one she would always have as the foundation to her existence.

Kayleigh shut the door softly and made her way down the stairs. In the kitchen, she turned on the light and made herself a cup of tea. The cottage was already cooling, despite having put the heating on extra late to welcome them when they returned home after the busy evening. By then, Emily had already been asleep in her wheelchair for some time. It had made it easier for Kayleigh to tidy up the store around her before heading back.

As she sat, brooding over her actions, she looked at the stack of papers in front of her. Just a few days ago, those same ones were enough to reduce her to a sweeping vortex of black misery. Now, at the thought of Maddy and her rescue, thanks to Jo and her endearing knight in shining armour routine, she realised they instead offered her a new bright spot in her life.

Perhaps they could just be friends? No, that was a terrible idea. You don't share a kiss with someone like that and then just act like it never happened. She might not have much experience with relationships in general and women in particular, but she was fairly certain it didn't work that way. Jo wanted more from her than that, even if she couldn't quite yet bring herself to imagine just what that was.

Whatever it was that she was avoiding, she knew it didn't sit well with the fact she had a secure thing going here. Boring. Responsible. Full of grown-up decisions. She'd seen the way Jo and Maddy had been with each other. She knew now that Jo was a few years younger than she was. That late twenties age when you should be enjoying yourself, not planning trips to the consultant for prosthesis measurements. The constant cajoling of wheelchairs and walking sticks. She was already doing that at the other end of the spectrum, so why the hell would she double up the responsibility and take it on here too?

As she sipped on her tea, she tried her best to ignore the fact that these were all her arguments, not Jo's. When she had walked into the shop that first time, she hadn't had a clue about Kayleigh's life, she was sure of that. But by the second time she had been in the store — and then almost unceremoniously thrown out of it afterwards — she knew all about Emily and her role in Kayleigh's life. That hadn't stopped her from continuing to help, to try and make things better for them, even when she had no real reason to do so. Even when it might cost her the job that she so badly needed. Those weren't small things. Nor were they ones taken blindly and without the knowledge of what it would mean if things ever got this far.

The memory of that kiss came back to her and she allowed herself to replay it in her mind. It had been perfect. Romantic. Romance was not a word she had come to associate with her life. Not for the first time, she wished Debra was here to talk to. She looked up at the picture on the wall. Her sister, smiling with Jack, never answered and never would. Over the years she had asked her so many questions about what she should do. They were always questions about Emily. Or the shop. Questions that she already knew the answer to, somewhere deep inside. This was different.

Debra would not have wanted her to spend her life alone. That much she knew. But it was easy to make those kinds of pronouncements when it was just your sister's happiness at stake. Not when it directly impacted the life of your daughter.

Emily had somehow already become attached to Jo. Even more so to Herbert. What would happen if the two of them got together and it didn't work out? How would she even explain the getting together, let alone the breakup? Hadn't Emily already been through so much? Having her world turned upside down as another adult she loved left her behind forever was far too much for Kayleigh to ever risk.

Emily had to come first. She drained her cup. The decision had been made, even if it hurt her to do so. She would explain it all to Jo, rationally and calmly, when she next saw her.

If she saw her, she thought, as she loaded the empty cup into the dishwasher. The way she had disappeared after the kiss, she wouldn't be surprised if Jo had got the message loud and clear. The business with the council over, she had no reason to see her again. Kayleigh wouldn't blame her if she just cut her losses and moved on, like any sensible person would.

She turned off the light and began to make her way back up to bed. As she did so, she looked around the room and saw the picture of her sister once again. For the first time, a mirage in the darkness, the face in the frame seemed to tell her she was doing the wrong thing.

CHAPTER SIXTEEN

Jo had left for work early that morning. She had no desire whatsoever to be there, but the decrepit building with its old windows and shoddy internet seemed to suit her mood more than home. It also didn't have her father, who had been willing at breakfast to pick up his questioning more or less exactly where he had left off the night before.

He had still been talking to his old cricket friend when she had walked back after the kiss. Unlike when she had left, he wasn't absorbed enough in the conversation not to notice her. From across the room, before she even reached him, his eyes met hers and she saw the concern flash across his face.

That had, somehow, been all the response she needed to know she must be looking as bad as she felt. Which, in that moment, was pretty bloody awful.

It had been a risk, she knew that. But she hadn't expected to blow it quite so badly. The memory of Kayleigh looking horrified by what they had done had continued to flash through her mind for the remainder of the evening and a good chunk of the night too. Sleep had been elusive and whenever it seemed she was about to drop off, seeing Kayleigh put her hand to her mouth in shock and shame before doing her best impression of an Olympic sprinter woke her right back up again.

They'd managed to avoid each other for the rest of the evening. Jo wasn't sure just who was avoiding who at that point, but her father had acquiesced without too much pushing when she suggested they leave early to beat the worst of the traffic out of the car park. She felt guilty for the insinuation that it was because of his wheelchair that added to their burden, but if he saw through it or was offended by it, then he let it slide.

Until they were in the car. There, sealed away from the rest of the world while the old fans blew cold air on them as she attempted to defrost the windows, his questions began in earnest. It was bad enough that the kiss had gone so badly wrong. She didn't need to describe the debacle to her own father. He didn't need to think about her kissing people. So she studiously avoided his questions, his concerns, and just told him that whatever they both hoped might happen definitely had not. Nor was it ever likely to.

She made herself a cup of terrible office coffee and sat down at her desk. She'd had plenty of failed seduction attempts, but this one was by far the worst. Perhaps being sober was where she had gone wrong? All her other completely obtainable crushes tended to go up in flames after a night of too much booze, usually egged on by Maddy.

That was it. She picked up her phone, took a sip of coffee and winced, then selected the number from her favourites list. Maddy picked up after a couple of rings. 'Can you talk?' Jo asked.

'Unless something has changed dramatically with my mouth since I last checked. Nope, they were definitely words. I can still talk. I appreciate your concern.'

'Quit being a smart ass.'

'What do you expect me to do? I'm on site, it's pissing it down like God's got a bladder problem and you're ringing me up to gloat. I can barely move after the other day.'

'Why would I be ringing you up to gloat?'

'Wasn't it the charity thingy last night? Did you put the twenty in the box from me like I asked you to?'

'I did.' Jo had put it in alongside a couple for herself and her father, even though she knew that Maddy wouldn't remember to pay up the next time they met. 'But why would I be gloating about that?'

'Well, I assume it all went off without a hitch thanks to my stunning repair work with the electrics, the whole village turned up, it was a fantastic success, Kayleigh looked into your eyes in wonder and gratitude and you both get to live happily ever after. I, on the other hand, ended up on the worst date ever last night and I'm not sure my knee will ever be the same again.'

'What did you do to your knee?'

'Are you sure you want to know? Because no amount of brain bleach will get the image out of your head once I tell you.'

'On second thoughts then, maybe not. Anyway, you're wrong about last night.'

'Shit, did something happen? It wasn't the electrics was it? I swear I did a good job. I mean, I know it was a little bit rushed, but I didn't cut any corners.'

'The electrics were fine. You saved the day.'

'Thank god for that. Then what was it? Nobody turned up? Old buggers too tight to part with their hard-earned cash to help the tiny kids?'

'No, you were right about the rest of it. All up until the happily ever after part. I stuffed it up.'

'How on earth did you stuff it up? After I went to the trouble of saving your ass.'

'I don't know. I thought that we were on the same page. After what Rob had said, I thought that she might be into me. But perhaps I got it wrong. Perhaps he meant something else entirely and I ended up kissing a straight woman.'

'Wouldn't be the first time.'

'Not helpful.'

'Scaring off straight women is practically your MO. But chill, I saw her. She was definitely into you.'

'After everything you've talked me into over the years, do you really expect me to trust your judgement?'

'I may have made one or two errors in the past. Oh hold on,' Maddy stopped talking and the sound of a drill whirring made Jo snatch the phone away from her ear. 'Sorry about that. Realised I hadn't made any noise in the past five minutes. The boss is on the warpath today.'

'I'm sorry, you should go.'

'Sod that, he arrived late and we ended up getting soaked waiting for him when he realised he forgot the key. Bit too much Christmas cheer last night if you ask me. Anyway, I saw the way she looked at you. I caught her looking a couple of times when she didn't think anyone would notice. Once you'd finished destroying her Christmas, I think she started to like you a bit more. There was chemistry.'

'Chemistry? Fat chance.'

'What happened? I swear, Rob was telling you the right thing. So it must have been something else you did wrong. Maybe you just took her by surprise or something. It was meant to be a big night for her.'

'We were trying to talk but it was noisy. So we went to the back of the store. You know, behind that monstrosity of a Christmas tree.'

'Oooh, cosy. Smooth move.'

'That was her move, not mine. But we were there and she apologised for being so mad at me when I was just doing my job. I thought we'd buried the hatchet. God Mads, she was so close to me I think I just lost my brain for a second. I looked up and there was some mistletoe above and I just thought what the hell. So I kissed her.'

'Then what's the problem? This is the stuff of Hollywood blockbusters. If Hollywood ever remembered that lesbians exist for any purpose other than to act as an attraction to the male gaze.'

'Now's not the time to get political. I need you to fix my love life, not take on the establishment.'

'What do you want me to say? It sounds like you did exactly what I would have done. Which is usually the right thing. Excluding last night, obviously. That was a big mistake.'

'If it was the right thing then why did she look horrified and run away?'

'Oh. That doesn't sound good. What did she say?'

'That it was a mistake that shouldn't have happened.'

'Ouch.'

'Exactly.'

'Did you kiss her in a normal way? Or did you do something weird? Because if you did something weird…'

'I don't even know what that means. Of course it was normal. I kissed her. She didn't pull away. In fact, I swear she was the one who pulled me into her, not the other way around. Then she did a complete one-eighty and ran for her life. We didn't speak again for the rest of the evening.'

'That sounds like more than just a problem with the kiss. Are you sure that was all it was?'

'What else could it be?'

'I don't know.' Maddy paused and Jo could practically hear her thinking in the background. The drill sounded again, but whether she was actually fixing something or if it was for effect, Jo couldn't tell. 'You know, when I got there the other morning, she was pretty messed up.'

'What do you mean?'

'I know it was early and believe me, we both looked like we needed the caffeine, but she seemed really upset. Puffy eyes, tired face, the works. Like she'd spent the night crying. I don't know, but I got the feeling it was about more than just the Christmas display. It was obvious she cared about that a whole lot too, but I got the feeling there was more going on. That it wasn't the only thing she had on her mind right then.'

'Perhaps there was something wrong with Emily?'

'Perhaps. I don't know. All I'm saying is that maybe you kissing her was just the final straw.'

'That may be the least flattering thing you've ever said to me. And the competition is pretty stiff.'

'I'm not saying kissing you causes women to have a nervous breakdown. I wouldn't necessary rule it out either, but I'll give you a free pass on it this time. I just meant that if she's got all that other stuff going on, then kissing you might have been too much for her to handle right at that moment. From everything you've said, she's spinning a lot of plates whilst being a saint. That's got to take its toll sooner or later.'

'I suppose you could be right.' Jo felt the glimmer of hope start to appear. It wasn't much and Maddy might not even be right, but it was better than anything she'd been able to come up with alone in the darkness. 'But what do I do now?'

'Go see her, dumbass.'

'The last thing she wants is to see me. If she wanted to see me then she would have stayed around last night.'

'She had plenty of other things to do last night other than worry about your ego. You need to go and see her. Not at the shop in the middle of the day when she's too busy. Give her an excuse and she'll take it. You know what women are like. Plus she's clearly way smarter than you, so it won't take much to pull the wool over your eyes.'

'Are you done with the insults for today yet?'

'I'm not sure. We'll see how it goes. Anyway, drop by the shop at the end of the day. Or perhaps you can go to her house. You can get her home address from your computer, right?'

'I think that's considered a criminal breach of the data protection act.'

'Your love life is on the line. The ends justify the means. Or you could just ask someone. Whatever. But get her when she won't have a readymade reason to escape.'

'And what am I supposed to do when I corner her like a crazed and jilted stalker?'

'Jeez, do I need to do everything for you? How have you got to twenty-seven and not learnt a single thing about women?'

'This is the first decent one I've got to that you haven't ruined first,' Jo shot back. 'Cut me some slack.'

'And there she is. I was starting to worry I'd lost you this morning. Think about it. She's been through hell.

Literally. Can you imagine going through something like that? I sure can't. To top it all off, she's got the kid to look after and it seems like the two of them have come through the other side of it all. That kid is in a good place and you know that's just because of whatever Kayleigh has done for her. You can't just expect to kiss her and suddenly become the centre of her world.'

'I didn't want to be the centre of her world. I just didn't want her to freak out.'

'Tell her that. You have to let her know that you're really into her. That this isn't just going to be a short fling. Hey, it's not is it? Because if it is, then don't go there. You know me, I'm all for a bit of fun, but now I've met her, that's not going to be what she needs. Don't go breaking her heart.'

'I've never broken anyone's heart. I wouldn't know how. And no, it's not just some one night stand I'm after. I really like her. Emily too.'

'That's what you've got to make her believe then. That if she goes on a date with you, if it turns into something more, then you're not going to mess that up.'

'Am I crazy?'

'Well I wouldn't want to take on someone else's family, but you're less selfish than I am. You know that whatever happens it won't be easy, right?'

'I know.'

'But you think it's worth it?'

'I really do.'

'Then that's what you have to tell her, not me. Damn, I really have to go.'

'Okay. And thanks.'

'No worries. Let me know how it goes. And remember, don't stuff it up this time. Later.' The line went dead and Jo put the phone down. The remains of her coffee had already gone cold, something that didn't do anything to improve the taste.

It didn't matter. Last night she had been in the depths

of despair, but now it seemed like there might be a logical explanation after all.

Knowing the problem might be more than just the fact she was a terrible kisser cheered her up, but that didn't mean what to do next was going to be quite as straightforward as Maddy made it sound. She'd tried to convince plenty of women to have a second date with her, but none of them had as much to lose as Kayleigh. In truth, Jo wasn't sure she had anything she could offer her that would entice her away from the life she had built for herself over the past three years. She was gainfully employed, but that was about it. And so far, that employment hadn't exactly been the thing that smoothed the path for them. Kayleigh had her own business, a child, and the venerable position as village guardian angel. Jo felt like an amateur at adulting in comparison.

She wiggled the mouse to bring the computer back to life and pulled up the screen to check for Kayleigh's home address. Just in time, she stopped herself. No, if she was going to do this, then she was going to do things right. Breaking the law was not the way to convince someone that you were genuine and to be trusted.

The end of the day seemed a long time away. If she managed to get any work done it would be a miracle. At least it gave her time to really think about what she was going to say. If she could get to the bookstore just before closing time, then she would have to convince Kayleigh to let her stay once the other customers were gone and the door was locked.

She twiddled a pencil between her fingers. If she could get her to do that, then there was a chance that Kayleigh would be willing to listen. As long as she made sense and didn't say the wrong thing, then there was a hope she would be able to convince her after all.

CHAPTER SEVENTEEN

With the stress of the charity night behind her, Kayleigh felt more relaxed than she had done since the beginning of December. As soon as the first day of that month rolled around, everything built up to boiling point. The anniversary, the charity fundraiser, the end of term chaos that Emily bought with her. Christmas day itself came with specific challenges, but the bulk of the stress came from the other events. With the added nightmare of getting the shop brought up to code at the very last minute this year, it was no wonder she felt like a weight had been lifted from her shoulders.

As long as she kept the memory of the previous night's kiss from her mind, she could just begin to relax.

As she rang another few books through the till and handed them over, she glanced up at the clock. 5:51. It was quiet on the high street as people walked, head down, keen to get home. The rain had eased off, leaving a faint fog lingering under the street lamps. The depths of winter were upon them, but inside the shop it felt warm and safe. Only a handful of customers remained and none of them seemed to be moving with any sense of urgency.

Her back ached from the cleanup operation. By the time she had opened that morning, all the tables had been moved to their proper positions and refilled with books. It was hard to believe that so many people had fit in amongst them the previous evening, but there were no traces of them now. Only the Christmas tree remained as a reminder and she was resolutely not looking at it.

She knew that she should enjoy it instead of letting it be a reminder of Jo and her soft lips. It was one of the main contributors to creating the delightful 'night before Christmas' atmosphere, so distinctly pleasant in comparison to the last-minute shopping mania of the main mall out of town. This was what her father and grandfather had always wanted their shop to be and the proud tradition she had vowed to continue. She rolled her shoulders, determined to enjoy every second of it if it killed her.

The bell above the door tinkled and she looked up, prepared to tell whoever it was that they were closing in just a few minutes, so unless they knew exactly what they were looking for then she was afraid they would have to leave. The words dried up on her lips when she saw Jo standing there, two gifts in her hands. She opened her mouth to say something — anything — but no words came out.

'Aunty Webby, it's Jo,' Emily pointed out helpfully.

'I can see that.'

'She doesn't have much time left to buy a book.' Emily's tone was completely serious. She hadn't got to grips fully with understanding a clock, but she knew that when one hand pointed right up and the other pointed right down, then it was time for the shop to close.

'I'm not sure she's here to buy a book,' Kayleigh murmured, her chance to send her away already past. She was inside and the door was closed behind her. She pushed the confusing rush of emotions aside. It didn't help that Jo was once again dressed in the casual clothes of outside the office, rather than her official looking council suit and coat. To top it off, a Santa hat was positioned on her head at what could only be described as a jaunty angle, making her look doubly cute. If she'd been dressed like that the first time she had walked through the door, Kayleigh would have made an effort to make sure she got a very special kind of customer service.

She pushed the thought rapidly from her head, her mind playing for the first time exactly what that might look like and feeling wholly inappropriate for doing so. A blush spread across her cheeks, she knew it. The whole room had suddenly become very hot. 'That's it folks,' she said, her voice cracking. 'We're closing up for Christmas.'

'You have to come to the till now.' Emily waved frantically at the few customers who had books in their hands. 'It's the rules.'

Even the stony faced teenager at the back of the room broke into a smile at Emily's over-serious sales approach. He joined the other few people in line as Kayleigh processed their sales with a practiced ease. The years of routine served her well, because her mind was most certainly not on the task in hand. Instead, it scrambled for all the reasons why she should tell Jo to leave with the rest of them. There seemed no way to do it without upsetting Emily — or making her ask a thousand questions at least — so with each customer she served, she felt a moment of truth looming down upon her.

When the last person took their bags, only Jo remained. She had been speaking to Emily, the two of them discussing something in hushed voices that Kayleigh couldn't quite make out, but she suspected might have something to do with the presents in her hand.

'Can we talk?' Jo asked, when she realised that everyone else was gone.

'Sure.' Kayleigh forced herself to sound casual, despite the churning in her stomach. 'I just need to lock up and then I'll be right back.'

'Take all the time you need.'

Those words seemed to be a lifeline and Kayleigh had no shame in using it. She took extra care in locking the door, taking the time to slowly turn the sign over to let everyone know they were closed, and pulling down the blind with excruciating care. In those precious extra seconds, she tried to work out what she could say to let Jo down more gently than she had done the night before.

She wasn't exactly proud of her disappearing act. In hindsight, it wasn't the most grown-up thing she could have done. If Jo was getting impatient, she showed no signs of it. By the time Kayleigh got back to the sales desk,

Jo was sitting on the floor next to Emily, looking so at home it almost broke her heart.

'Hi,' she said softly, making Jo look up. It was as close to a peace offering she could give.

'Hi.'

'Merry Christmas.'

'Merry Christmas to you too. I brought you both a gift. It's nothing big. I thought we might be able to talk.'

'I have to finish up here first. Is that okay?'

'I can help you if you want? We can walk and talk at the same time.'

'Sure.' Kayleigh swallowed nervously. It wasn't ideal, but at least it would give her something to do with her hands. She had no idea what Jo was going to say, or if she was even ready to hear it, but now they were both here it seemed too late to turn her away. 'Emily, do you need anything? Or can you play here while we get everything finished? We won't be long, I promise.'

'I can stay here.' Emily gave her most innocent smile, but Kayleigh could see right through it. The present from Jo remained wrapped at her side, but that wouldn't stop her from squeezing and feeling once they were gone to try to guess what it was.

'No opening.'

'I won't.'

'Not even a corner. Promise?'

'I promise.'

'Good girl.' Kayleigh moved away from the counter and she heard Jo get up from the floor behind her.

'What do you need me to do?'

'I have to turn all the Christmas lights off and pull the tables in away from the doorway. Over Christmas I tend to pull the blinds in the windows a third of the way closed, but not all the way down. Then we have to count the takings and put them upstairs in the safe. I hate to do it, but I never make it to the bank in time for the last day.'

'But it's not all in there, is it?'

'No. I took most of it mid-afternoon so I could see Rob before he finished for the day.'

'Did you tell him about last night?'

'No.' She had wanted to. Really wanted to. But talking about it would make it real. She got the feeling he would also have told her off for being so foolish and she hadn't been quite ready to hear that yet. No one should have to defend themselves on Christmas Eve against charges of romantic stupidity.

'Oh.'

'I needed some time. To think.'

'And what have you come up with?' Jo took the other end of the table and lifted it with her. Between them they carried it backwards a few feet, out of the immediate path from the doorway.

'I'm not sure.' The silence stretched out again as they moved the second table. It still felt too close to Emily's careful ears to be having a deep and meaningful grown-up discussion. She indicated they should move to the far corner of the room to begin unplugging the lights. It wasn't exactly a two man job, but she had a feeling that had nothing to do with why Jo was helping.

'I hope you don't mind that I brought her a gift?'

'No. Not at all. That was very sweet of you.'

'I kept the receipt. In case it was something you'd already brought.'

'Don't you mean Santa?' Kayleigh gave her a grin, even though they were now out of earshot. 'What did you get her anyway?'

'An action figure. One of the new superhero ones. She seemed so taken with the idea of my dad being a superhero in his wheelchair, I thought it might be nice for her to see girls could be superheroes too. No matter what.'

'That's very thoughtful of you.' Kayleigh felt a lump in her throat. A gift from a woman who was clearly trying to convince her that they should date was hardly a surprise. But the thought behind it was something else.

'She's a good kid. You've done a great job with her.'

'That's all her, not me. She's tough.'

'Don't sell yourself short. I can't imagine how difficult it must have been for you in the circumstances. You've given her the best start she can, despite a pretty rubbish situation. I think your sister would be proud of you.'

'Thank you.' Kayleigh bent down to unplug another set of lights, using the distraction to brush away a stray tear that had fallen. People said that to her all the time, but it was nothing more than a platitude in most instances. Words from people who had never known her sister and didn't know what else to say. She knew they always meant to be kind, but most of the time it sounded hollow. Jo sounded sincere. The words both elated and wounded at the same time. 'She means everything to me.'

'I know. Despite what you might think, I understand that.'

'You might believe that you do, but you've only seen us together a couple of times. Here. When everything is okay. We're a package deal and that comes with as much bad as it does good.'

'No kid is perfect all the time. I might not have much experience with them, but I do know that much.'

'Emily has additional challenges on top of just being over-tired sometimes. They're not going to disappear.'

'Emily is strong. Not to mention brave. Look at her. Really look at her. I've never known a kid with such a sense of themselves and their independence. She's like that because you allowed her to be. You've given her the courage and confidence to be whoever she wants to be. It's not some stupid toy that will make her believe she can be a superhero. It's the lessons that you've taught her that will make her believe that.'

'I'm not sure how it would even work with someone else.' Kayleigh looked up and for the first time, stared directly into Jo's eyes. She had to let her know that she wasn't just being afraid. Over-cautious. These were very real problems. The woman standing in front of her didn't flinch or look away. Instead, Kayleigh found a hand slipping into hers.

'I have no idea either. I'm not going to make any promises about the future. How can I? We hardly got off to the best start. One kiss and you ran for the hills,' Jo smiled to take some of the sting out of her words. 'So I won't say anything just because I think it would convince you. I know that if we let whatever this is between us become something more, then there will be some tough times ahead. I have no idea what the future holds, but I'm willing to try.'

'I'm not sure that's enough. The store and Emily take up all of my time. Not to mention energy. Once she goes to sleep I practically collapse each night. I have no idea how to date around that. Those things can't change. Emily can't come second to anything or anyone else.'

'I'm not asking you to. But you can't wait until she turns eighteen before you allow yourself to start seeing anyone. Have you even been on a single date since…' she trailed off, but she didn't have to specify when.

'Since the accident? No. There hadn't been many before the accident either. I'm not very good at the relationship thing. You're probably better off just walking away now.'

'I don't want to do that. Deep down, I don't think you want me to either.'

'I have too many responsibilities.' Kayleigh could feel the argument beginning to weaken under Jo's gaze.

'I never knew your sister, well, apart from one dinner hall incident I'll tell you about sometime, but I don't think she'd want you to have no life at all. She'd be so proud of you for looking after her child in the way you have. You've devoted your life to Emily. But I don't think she'd want you to have no happiness of your own. Do you?'

'I don't know.' The tears began to fall and this time she didn't even make a pretence at stopping them.

'I think you do. Did she know you liked women?'

'Of course. We told each other everything. She was my best friend as much as she was my sister.'

'Do you think she would have approved of you bringing her daughter up if you were in a relationship with another woman?'

'I don't think it would have bothered her as long as Emily was looked after.'

'So that's one thing you don't have to worry about. And if you know that much, then you also know the answer to the question of whether or not she would want you to be happy with someone.' Jo reached up and wiped the tears away.

'Damn you.' There was no malice in her voice. She had no idea how Jo had used her own word logic to work against her until she had no arguments left, but somehow she had.

With her fears shot down around her, she knew it left only two questions. Did she actually want to date a woman who had spent the majority of the time they had known each other infuriating the hell out of her? Jo gave her another smile of encouragement and she felt her stomach do a small flip. She did. It was terrifying to consider that another kiss like the one they had shared the previous evening might happen again so soon.

But there was still question number two. Regardless of whether or not she wanted to try, Emily got final refusal.

'So how about it?' Jo asked, sensing she was on the brink of something. Kayleigh checked her watch. They really need to get a move on. Emily wouldn't continue to play quietly for much longer.

'Do you have any plans? I know it's Christmas Eve and you've probably already got something sorted but—'

'I have no plans. Not Christmas Eve plans. As long as I go home tonight and make sure that Dad has made it to bed okay, then I'm all yours. If you want me.'

'Emily and I have our own Christmas Eve traditions.'

That first Christmas they had spent together, it had seemed important for her to establish them, even though Emily had been far too young to understand. She wanted to set them in stone before she herself had a chance to forget what her family Christmases were meant to be. What they would have been like if things had been different. That Christmas Eve, the two of them had spent it alone, just as they had done every Christmas since. She didn't know what made her extend the offer to Jo, but somewhere deep inside it felt right. It could be time to share it with someone else who would make the time special in a different way.

'If you're sure?' Jo seemed to understand the enormity of what she was saying. Kayleigh was grateful she didn't push.

'It's not up to me. But if Emily is okay with it, then perhaps you could come home with us for a few hours?' She was careful to make sure the offer didn't extend into the night. One step at a time. This already felt more than her heart could handle.

'I'd love to.'

'In that case, we'd better go and ask.' Kayleigh didn't break their hands apart as she led Jo over to the counter, where the rustle of paper told her that Emily was still trying to work out exactly what the gift was. Before they reached there, she stopped and turned around. 'If she says no, then that's it. I won't push her and I won't let you do it either. A hint that you're trying to convince her and that's it.'

'I wouldn't dream of it.'

'Good.' Feeling better that she had made some small step towards laying unfamiliar ground rules, she continued to where Emily sat. 'That present better not have even a millimetre of paper torn, missy.'

'It hasn't. I promise.'

'Good. Because it's not too late for Santa to change his mind about his naughty list.'

'I've been good. I want to be on the good list.' There was a hint of mild panic in her voice. Kayleigh suppressed a smile. This time of year had fabulous blackmail material to get things done. 'Well as long as you carry on being good before bed then I think you'll be on it. I have a question for you.'

'Yes?'

'How would you feel if Jo came back to the house with us for Christmas Eve?' Kayleigh wasn't sure if she had worded the question right, but this was all a new and steep learning curve. Had she given Emily enough wiggle room to say no if that was what she really wanted?

'Can she?' Emily scrabbled up from the floor, excitement lighting up her eyes.

'If you want her to.'

'Yes, we can show her our Christmas tree there too. It's not as big as this one,' she confided, taking Jo's other hand, 'but I think it's just as pretty.'

'Wow, that must be really pretty then,' Jo said, crouching down until she was eye level with Emily. Kayleigh watched, hardly daring to breathe. 'But I can come and see it another time if you want to spend tonight just with your aunt. I know it's a special time of year.'

'No, that's okay. I want to show you the tree. Can she have a mince pie too?' Emily looked up at Kayleigh.

'I think so.'

'They're special ones. From granny's recipe.'

'I'm sure they taste amazing.'

'They do. I don't like mince pies but granny's mince pies are special. She's dead too like Mommy and Daddy. At Christmas eve, they look down and watch us eat them instead.'

'I bet they're all very pleased that you enjoy them then. I'm sure I will too.' There was a hitch in Jo's voice but she controlled it well. Kayleigh felt herself doing the familiar trick of pushing her fingernails into her palm until the crescents almost drew blood. The physical pain always helped hold the emotional pain, and the visible tears that Emily would see, at bay.

'In that case,' Kayleigh jumped to Jo's rescue, 'we'd better get things finished here. I'll just get the money up to the safe and then we can go. Start putting your coat on.' She gave Jo a little squeeze on the shoulder as she walked past. If this thing, whatever it was, was going to work between the two of them, then she wouldn't always be able to provide a distraction from the casual trauma of Emily's life. But tonight, Jo had met the test and that was enough of a start.

As she climbed the stairs to the upstairs room that housed the stock and the safe, the sounds of Emily filling in Jo on their Christmas Eve traditions drifted up to her ears. She had no idea if she was doing the right thing. It was hard. Hard enough that it made complete sense as to why she had been putting it off all these years. Too busy to be lonely, why put herself through all this added stress as well?

But now the option was out there and the memory of this kiss meant it would not easily go away. Tonight, once Emily had finally been persuaded to go to bed, then there was every chance that kiss would happen again. If it had been anything like the first, then Kayleigh knew she would not want it to stop.

As she placed the money into the safe, she felt the terrible weight of uncertainty fill her again. She'd built her life so carefully, with so many spaces that no one else could go. Even up here, a simple stock room held so much family sentimental significance that no one else was allowed in. The temporary staff collected the stock she had chosen from the bottom of the stairs once she had carried it down. Books had become walls to her and with each wall that was crumbling, the future seemed less and less certain.

In her dreams and her nightmares, she had walked the road that lay ahead of her countless times. The road that took Emily through primary school, where her friends knew her and never cared about the fact she had a prosthesis that meant she used a wheelchair sometimes. Secondary school filled her with more fear, when teenagers were cruel just to be cruel sometimes, and Emily would have a reason to stand out. In her more positive moments she allowed her hopes for the future go beyond that, to university and a career. A doctor, a lawyer, usually something more driven that Kayleigh would have chosen for herself. Any dream profession that showed Emily could do just as well as any fully able-bodied person would.

None of those dreams had ever included anyone else walking with them through the journey. It would take a long time for Jo to fall in step with them, in the present and in the future.

As she turned to take one last look at the room, a final procrastination before facing the future, something caught her eye. There, in the loosely defined children's section, a book poked its spine out further from the rest. An old edition of *Charlotte's Web* that she always hesitated to put out for sale. Its gloss cover glinted at her in the faint light and she smiled. Like a ghost of Christmas past, it was the closest thing she was going to get to a sign.

If her sister thought everything would be okay, then the least she could do was try.

GET FREE STUFF!

To sign up to my mailing list and receive sneak previews, free novellas and other updates, visit ckmartin.com/free-stuff

ABOUT THE AUTHOR

C.K. Martin is a British writer of mostly - but not exclusively - lesbian fiction. She loves writing character-driven stories, so you'll find her books in the romance, crime, thriller and fantasy genres. She believes that realistic, diverse and engaging characters shouldn't come at the expense of great plots - readers deserve to have both. If you enjoy her characters in one genre, then you'll find similar heroines in the others if you feel like branching out. Discover detectives, vampires, gangsters and runaways, all looking for their happy ending.

When she's not writing, she can usually be found with her nose in a book (or pressed against the Kindle screen). Her third biggest passion in life is travel, so although she's based in England, for much of the year you won't find her there. Instead she'll be hanging out with her wife in some amazing city or, more likely, at the beach.

You can get in touch with the author by email ckmartin.author@gmail.com, or follow on twitter @CKMauthor. For more frequent updates, visit http://www.ckmartin.com/

OTHER BOOKS AVAILABLE FROM

THIS AUTHOR

DIRTY LITTLE WAR
TAPAS AND TANGELOS
HAPPILY EVER AFTER THIS CHRISTMAS

TEDDIE MCKAY SERIES
THE CROCHET KILLER
A TASTE TO DIE FOR

URBAN FANTASY BOOKS (AS CAS MARTIN)
BLOOD INHERITANCE
BLACK MARKET BLOOD
SHADOWS OF BLOOD

11211116R00109

Printed in Great Britain
by Amazon